THE MADDY SAGA

BOOK ONE

MADDY BECOMES A PONYGIRL

BY

PAUL BLADES

Cover Art by Agnes Knox
agnesknox@simonas.se
agnes.knox@gmail.com

Dark Visions Publications
darkvisionspub@gmail.com

Watch for publication of the other books in the Maddy Saga:

Other books by Paul Blades:

Klitzman's Isle
Klitzman's Empire
Klitzman's Paradise
The Taking of Cheryl Part One
The Taking of Cheryl Part Two: Slaver's Bait
Comfort Girl No. 4
Sacrifice to the Emerald God
The Blue Cantina: Anna's Surrender

CHAPTER ONE

It was a typical Saturday afternoon at Grafton's Tavern. There were three sullen patrons at the semi-circular bar. The Tennessee game was on the television, and the home team was leading Miami by 10 points in the third quarter. Four of the Baker Hill boys were playing pool, drinking Coors and doing the occasional shot of Wild Turkey. Their mildly profane shouts were the only noise in the place audible over the nonstop chatter of the game announcers.

Madeline stood behind the bar, the cheeks of her young, firm ass resting on the large, silver colored beer cooler. She was a tall, well built girl, about 5'11". She wore a peasant style skirt with bright calico swirls that descended to well below her knees. Her top was a bright red, Moorestown Community College t-shirt, pulled taut across her chest, accentuating her more than ample breasts. Her hair was long and auburn, reaching to her waist. While working, she kept it bound tightly in a braid, a bright pink ribbon serving as a tie on the end. Madeline wore her low top cross trainers; she was conscious of her towering height and shunned anything that would add more than a quarter inch to her frame. The shoes were kind to her feet too. Along with her height came a comparable weight, although she dieted constantly. Broad shoulders and big bones separated her from the lithe, tall fashion model types. But she was pretty, had a distinctly feminine shape and was lively and fun to be around. Her face and arms were brown still from her spring break foray to Florida and her muscles were taut and well toned.

Two of the men at the bar were regulars. Danny ran the garage across the street, and on Saturdays he closed up at noon, or three, depending on whether Tennessee was playing an early or late afternoon basketball game. He was in his late fifties, was divorced, and had little visually to offer a young college girl like Madeline. His belly protruded over his blue work pants. His grease stained work shirt, of the same dark utilitarian color, spread open at the top to reveal a densely hairy, salt and pepper chest to match his scraggly beard. Old Grand Dad and Schlitz was what he drank. When the game was over, he would buy two sixes and head home.

Manny sat a few seats down from Danny. He was in his thirties, a lean, wiry fellow. He liked to think of himself as a lady's man and wore sharply creased beige pants and a bright yellow Izod shirt. His hair was slicked back in a mini pompadour and he liked to sport a day or two's growth on his face, kind of like one of those detectives on Miami Vice. He had money on Tennessee, but he had to give away 7 ½ points. His eyes were glued to the screen and cursed the Volunteers whenever the Hurricanes dropped one in the hoop.

The third fellow was someone who Maddy, everybody called her Maddy, had never seen before. He was nursing a 7 oz. glass of Bud draft and seemed preoccupied with himself. The man was maybe in his mid fifties, maybe older. He wore a dark blue baseball cap with a Caterpillar Bulldozer logo on the front. He wore a short, dark green work jacket zipped up over a white tee shirt, blue jeans and work shoes. His hair was short and gray, almost a buzz cut. Maddy wasn't sure how tall he was because he sat kind of hunched over, like he was trying not to be noticed. Well, neither Manny nor Danny seemed to have noticed him. And the Baker Hill boys were too involved in their afternoon away from their wives and girlfriends to have any interest.

Miami had just scored a three pointer that caught the Tennessee defenders flat footed. Manny cursed and pounded his fist on the bar. A quarter popped into the air and then rolled off, over the sink and down onto the floor by Maddy's feet. "Jesus fuckin' Christ on a cross!" Manny yelled. "Those stupid, fucking, hillbilly assholes!" Manny didn't bet much, maybe a twenty or a fifty on a game, but he was a cheap son-of-a-bitch and hated losing any money. He looked up at Maddy who had jumped at the sudden noise.

"Sorry, Maddy," he said. "I didn't mean to startle you."

"That's fine, Manny," she replied in her soft, deep toned voice. "But don't break the bar, o.k.?"

"Sure honey, sure," Manny replied. "Ah," he said to her somewhat meekly, "could you get my quarter?"

"A quarter saved is a quarter earned, eh, Manny," she joked.

"Yeah, I guess you've got that right." He watched as Maddy bent to retrieve his quarter. "I know I'm tight with a buck Maddy, but I don't mind spending it on the ladies. Now you, for instance, I'd spend that quarter on you in a New York minute, and a couple more too."

"Well, I'll just run home and get my pretty dress on, Manny. Where we going, the Piggly Wiggly or the Stop and Shop?"

"Honey, we can go anywhere you want as long as we end up at my place." Manny quipped back.

Maddy knew Manny was harmless. He talked a big game, but she had heard it from Sally Jensen that Manny was a little light where it counted. Anyway, she could take a little ribald ribbing. It was good for tips and made her feel just a little more attractive.

She crouched to her knees to find Manny's precious quarter. As she did so, her skirt pulled tight around her legs and buttocks. Her finely tapered thighs were outlined by the cloth. The man in the bulldozer hat took especial notice.

She stood up quickly and slapped Manny's quarter on the bar. "Here's your fuckin' 25 cents, Manny. Don't spend it all in one place," she told him. But Manny was already glued back to the T.V. screen. Tennessee had given away an offensive rebound to the Miami team and their forward had promptly slammed it into the basket.

"God fuckin damn it!" Manny yelled. "Of all the god damn, fuckin', stupid things to do! Jesus!"

Maddy returned to her perch on the beer cooler. She looked around. The man in the bulldozer cap was gone. He left a 35 cent tip.

The man in the bulldozer cap's name was Herman Rusch. As he drove his battered, green Ford pickup from the tavern parking lot, he made a little note in small, spiral memo pad: "Maddy, 21 or 22, tall, athletic. Pretty face, long, muscled legs, reddish-brown, waist length hair. Grafton's Tavern, Marlsburg, Saturday, 2:30 p.m." He always took notes, although he destroyed them later. It took a careful, observant man to ply his trade. Patience too. He pulled the truck out on to Cooperstown Road and headed south.

He had been looking for a girl like Maddy for a while. Three or four girls he had found had come close, but this one was just about right. He would talk it over with Louise, his wife, and work out a plan. They would need to know more about the girl: where she lived, what her habits were. Was she living at home? With a boyfriend?

There had been four pick up trucks and a small Ford Escort in the parking lot. Inside the Ford was a stuffed animal and a woman's sweater. There was a decal from Moorestown Community College on the rear window. The man felt it a safe assumption this was Maddy's car. He took the license plate number.

The other tall girls he had scoped out were more like string beans. He wasn't looking for the willowy type. The girl he was looking for had to be strong and shapely. And tall. Maddy was all three. Her torso was long and sleek, but her hips were wide. Her arms were far from delicate, and the thighs and ass were ample. She had luscious looking, heavy mounds on her chest. She would do fine.

Five hours later, Herman pulled off of Route 265 in Canterville, Georgia. It was dark now and he was tired. It was a lot of driving, but you couldn't shit where you ate. He had made many a long distance drive in his pursuit of female flesh, once even all the way to Pennsylvania. But he liked to keep his business limited to small town, Southern girls. In his inimitable redneck way, he loved to think of those snotty bitches getting fucked in the ass by some South American mongrel drug dealer or some greasy little Arab. It was all fantasy though, because he never met the ultimate customer. He dealt with middle men. And for two weeks he had been looking to fill a particular order. Maddy fit the bill to a 'T'.

As he coasted up his long, gravel strewn driveway, Herman thought about Louise. If he didn't need that fat, old witch to help snatch the girls and take care of them until they could be sold, he'd of put her in a hole a long time ago. When they were younger, she was a pip. She loved to fuck and raise hell. But now she cussed him and snarled anytime he put his hand on her. Was it any wonder that he had his way with the girls from time to time?

Herman pulled up to the porch of his ramshackle house. It was an old, wooden frame structure, with rotted out gutters and weeds sticking up all about the foundation. He and Louise had made plenty of money over the years, but they had to hold on to this decrepit shithole of a house if they wanted to stay in business. There was an old, red barn in the back. They needed the barn. And the location was hidden, at least two miles from the main road. Where could they ever find another place like this?

Louise heard Herman pull up and shot back the inch and a half of Southern Comfort she was drinking out of a jelly jar. "A little bit more money," she thought, "and I'll fix that asshole's wagon." Louise harbored her own resentments against Herman. She knew he liked to fool with the merchandise. That didn't bother her. It was more the way he looked at her with disdain. Sure, she had gotten old, what the fuck did he expect! But her pussy still worked at 54 years of age and she had the old urges from time to time. Now, when Herman was out prowling, she often forced oral delights from the girls locked in the cellar beneath the barn. In fact, just about an hour ago she had had a little session with that cunt, Sharon. She had a good, long tongue and preferred using it to the blast of a cattle prod.

Herman trudged up the front porch and entered the living room. Louise was right where he knew she would be, sitting in the easy chair in front of the T.V. The jelly glass didn't fool him. He knew where she kept the hootch, and besides he could smell it on her breath. "Goddam drunken sow!" he thought.

"So wadja get Herman?" Louise asked him. "Any luck?"

"Yeah," Herman replied, removing his cap and throwing it onto the brown, threadbare couch. "I think I've got a winner." He read off the description to Louise. She nodded.

"Seems like the one we need all right. When can you get the plate run?"

"Tomorrow. I'll call my contact and get her address in the morning. You should take the car up in the afternoon, see what you can find out. I'd like to get a picture, send it in. There's not much of a market for these big boned girls and I want to make sure that she fits the bill before we spend too much time on her. Meanwhile, we got that girl in Daleysville we could pick up, or the one in Jackson." Herman sighed, his exhaustion slowly beginning to overwhelm him.

"There's some meatloaf in the fridge and some potatoes on the stove," Louise proffered. "You want I should heat 'em up?"

"Nah," Herman replied. "I'm going to go check on the cunt down in the hole and then get to bed. I'm pretty tuckered."

Louise knew what 'checking on the cunt in the hole' meant. Herman would get a blow job and then go to bed. Well, fine by her.

"As you please," she replied.

Herman strode through the kitchen and out the back door. The barn was located behind the house, about 40 yards back. It was an old, weather beaten structure, with faded, red boards and peeling roof shingles. He knew he should get up there and fix them before the heavy, spring rains set in, but he had been thinking lately, maybe they had enough dough now to get out of here. A couple more scores and they would have over two million dollars. He would put a bullet in Louise's brainpan, dump her in the hole and take off for South America. Two million would go a long way there. And there was plenty of cheap pussy.

The half moon that was dodging through the clouds lit the pathway to the barn so that Herman was able to traverse the short distance without the use of a flashlight. He stepped into the barn and headed towards the back. A small pile of wooden pallets lay next to the rear wall. Herman carefully picked them up one by one and moved them aside. A small trap door appeared. The door had a lock on it and Herman keyed the lock and opened the steel bolt that held the door closed. He pulled the door up and advanced down a wooden ladder built into the wall, closing the trap door behind him. When he reached the bottom, he turned.

This was 'the hole'. It was a veritable dungeon. It was lit by a single 45 watt bulb in the ceiling in the center of the room. Along the right wall was a series of five cages. They stood about three feet high and four feet wide. Each cage had a wooden floor covered by a thin mat. In the first cage knelt a small, naked girl. Her silky blond hair was pulled back in a pony tail. She had sparkling blue eyes and pale skin. She was alert to the coming of Herman, her jailor. Her hands were connected by a short chain that led through a ring dangling from a steel collar around her neck. The chain held her hands in a prayer-like position, there being just enough slack for the girl to be able to cover one of her plump, firm breasts, but not the other, as the other hand would be drawn up close to her neck.

The girl wore no gag, it being unnecessary in this subterranean prison. The ceiling was insulated with sound deadening materials and the door to the below ground chamber was about six inches thick. You could set off a hand grenade in there and the only thing heard upstairs would be a dull thump, and that only if you were standing directly above it at the time.

Although not gagged, the girl knew enough to remain silent. She knew that this wasn't one of the regular visits from her captors, having been served her meager dinner only about an hour before. The beans and chopped up hotdogs had gone down quickly as the girl was fed just enough to meet her daily energy needs. Locked into a cage twenty-four hours a day, her needs were small. Most of the girls who were captured were a little overweight, and some caloric deprivation allowed some of that fat to burn off. Besides, it was better to have the girls' energy levels low. The less energy, the less trouble.

Not that they could make much. Their hands were rarely unlocked until the day they were displayed for their potential buyers. There was just enough play so that they could hold a bowl to their mouths. They had to rely on the graciousness of their jailors to wipe their asses and cunts after discharging bodily wastes. Imagine trying to climb a ladder with your hands locked under your chin. Even if you could do it, the lock to the trap door, which relocked automatically when it was shut, was on the side of the door farthest from the wall. There would be no way to reach it with your hands confined and held close to your body. There was also an alarm button which rang at the house and sent a message to Louise and Herman's cell phones. Whatever happened to one of them while in the 'hole', the other would be alerted that there was trouble. The keys to the cuffs were usually left in the house.

The girl's name was Sharon. Her last name is unimportant. She had been collected by Herman and Louise two days ago. It was an easy snatch, done right outside her apartment in Altoona. She parked right next to the van and when she had locked her car and started walking to her apartment, the van door slid open and she was pulled in. Herman was strong; no 120 lb. girl was a match for him. She was in the van with tape over her mouth before she knew what was happening. Louise had been standing by with the duct tape and, once it was applied to the girl's lips, jumped into the driver's seat, slowly eased the van out into the parking lot and then away.

There had been no need to knock Sharon out during the ride from Altoona to Herman and Louise's farm. Herman quickly subdued her and had bindings around her wrists behind her back and on her ankles. There was a compartment built in the side of the van just big enough to hold a gagged and bound female. There was almost no room for movement and it was heavily insulated. A small pump blew in fresh air while a small exhaust drew it out. Even if stopped by the police, unless the van was searched thoroughly, there was little risk of detection. Years ago, Herman had had a girl choke on her own vomit after knocking her out with chloroform. You never knew when was the last time the girls ate. He would not risk it again.

For two days the 19 year old Sharon had knelt shivering with fear in the dim, damp cold of her prison. She remembered well the sensation of being lowered head first down the stairs, her eyes covered with a blindfold. She remembered being stripped and collared, the bracelets affixed to her hands, the confining link between them established. She had cowered, naked, kneeling at the feet of her kidnappers, too afraid to beg for freedom. The first night, all that had happened was that her breasts and belly were manhandled a bit by the man, his rough, calloused hands scraping her tender skin. She had felt the bite of the cattle prod the next day when she had refused to eat. She felt it again when she had broken down and whined and pleaded to be released. And she had felt it a third time when she protested, meekly, the need to use the small trough below her cage for her wastes. She had learned to avoid punishment at all costs.

On the second day, the man had dragged her head through a small hinged and locked window in the cage and fastened her by the back of the neck to the cage's top. He pulled out his wizened dick and commanded her to suck it. With tears in her eyes she had complied.

The old lady had left her alone until this morning. It was the woman who wiped her ass and her vagina, three times a day. Her nerves had loosened her bowels to a liquid discharge. The old lady brought food and filled the water bottle strung above the cage's top. Just enough of a nozzle peeped into the cage that Sharon could fix her lips on it and suck the water out, like a hamster. It was Louise who had twice given Sharon a taste of the cattle prod.

This morning, Sharon sensed that something was up. The old man had been in early and gotten a blow job from her. The woman, who Sharon assumed was the old man's wife, was a hefty, almost corpulent woman. She had strong arms and legs and broad shoulders, as if she had done heavy physical labor all of her life. She had brownish gray hair, drawn back into a bun. Her eyes were sunken deep in her face, which was long and narrow. Her chin jutted out and there was a huge mole on her face just to the right and above her nostrils. Years of hard living had carved their punishment on her face.

She had been curt and brusque with Sharon, telling her to retrieve her dinner bowl or ordering her to turn around so that her rear and cunt could be attended to. This morning, after wiping the twin openings and applying a soothing lotion there, the old lady's hand remained, stroking Sharon's pussy. Sharon was bent over, her head on the mat that served as a floor to the cage, her legs spread. She knew not to display any resistance to the old lady, who seemed more than twice her size. And she always carried the cattle prod, or had quick access to it.

The hand gently petted the twin lips surrounding her love channel and she felt fingers lightly playing with the little nub at the top. Against her own will, Sharon's pussy began to lubricate. As it did, the woman inserted her fingers deep inside, probing, rubbing against the top and walls of the vagina. Sharon let out a little squeak as feelings of mortification and shame overcame her. Was this why she was being held? Would the sexual abuse get more and more demanding until she became the old couple's sexual plaything?

Sharon could not help but notice the presence of five other cages. She could not but wonder at the elaborate hideaway. Something darker than mere sexual abuse awaited her. She felt it, knew it, but could not believe it.

The woman pulled her hand from Sharon's moist divide just at the moment when Sharon issued an involuntary moan of sexual excitement. The old lady slapped her ass hard and demanded that she turn around. She was pulled by her hair from her cage, the first time she had been out of it since she arrived, and dragged onto the floor. The old lady pushed Sharon down on her back and fastened a rope around each of her ankles, spreading them apart, and tying them off on some rings in the floor. Then she pulled up her skirt and with a practiced effort, removed her large, white, cotton panties. She lowered herself until she was kneeling with Sharon's torso between her knees. The old lady leaned over until her face was inches from Sharon's.

"Have you ever sucked a cunt, dearie?" she hissed, her stale breath pouring over Sharon's face. Sharon shook her head fearfully. She never had and never wanted to. She had let her boyfriend do it, once.

"Well you're going to do it now. And you're going to lick it and suck on my clit until I come all over your face! And you better be good, girlie, or I'll stick the wand up your twat and pull the trigger!"

Sharon mewed piteously, but nodded her head in affirmation. The old woman swung her legs around so that she was facing Sharon's feet, placed her knees on either side of Sharon's neck and slowly lowered her dark, bushy divide on Sharon's face. Sharon felt its wetness smear across her nose and over her lips. The woman pressed down hard, her skirt bunched around her waist. "Suck it, you no good slut!" she yelled. "Suck my cunt!"

Sharon tentatively stuck her tongue into the steaming, hot morass that covered her face. She tasted the pungent secretions that had already begun to flow. Slowly, with disgust and revulsion, she moved her tongue back and forth.

Louise felt the tentative probe of her hole by the girl. She was impatient. She leaned forwards slightly. She always kept a small quirt on the belt to her dress when she came to visit the prisoners. She pulled it out now and came down with it hard at the apex of Sharon's thighs.

"Aieeeee!" Sharon cried out, her voice muffled by the female flesh pressed onto her face. Louise struck it again.

"Aieeeee!" Sharon screamed again. Her legs strained at their bindings in an effort to cover up her vulnerable sex.

"Get licking, you lazy bitch or I'll give you ten more of these!" Louise yelled.

Sharon began licking the messy cunt now with alacrity. Tears were flowing down her face as she could still feel the sting of the lashes that had bit down on her tender love lips. Louise, satisfied now with the efforts of the captive, began to moan and sigh as she rocked her hips on Sharon's mouth. She pressed the tip of her cunt into Sharon's oral cavity. "Suck on my clit, you whore, suck on it!" she commanded.

The frightened girl sucked hard on the stiff nub of flesh. Louise moaned loudly as she pressed it harder against

Sharon's mouth. She eyed the jewel between Sharon's widespread legs. She was no lesbian, she told herself, but she had developed a taste for pussy over the years, young, fresh pussy. She leaned over and, spreading her own legs wider, took possession of Sharon's sex with her lips. Sharon jolted with surprise as she felt the hot lips enflame her clit. She futilely tried to close her legs, to prevent this abuse of her private place. But her ankles had been tied firmly apart and her struggles only enflamed Louise more.

Sharon's entire head was covered with Louise's dress, blocking out almost all light, like a shroud. She was glad she couldn't see; glad that she could forgo almost all visual stimuli during this humiliating assault. She felt Louise's tongue probe between her now engorged pussy lips and moaned into the messy cunt that covered her face. Louise spread the girl's lower lips wider apart with her hands and licked the musky organ its entire length. Sharon felt the rough tongue of the woman tormenting her sex and moaned again, all the while feverishly seeking to drive the older woman to her pinnacle of pleasure. Juice flowed down her face from the oozing crevasse. Louise was rubbing it harder and harder against her lips. Sharon could feel her own blood stirring, a wave of pleasure about to burst over her. She did not want it, but she couldn't stop it. When she heard Louise issue a long, deep groan and press her thighs tightly against her cheeks, Sharon at last gave in to the relentless lips and tongue between her thighs and cried out, bucking her hips, clenching her fists, straining at the chains that bound her hands and the ropes that bound her legs.

After her waves of pleasure subsided, Louise rose from the girl's prone body. She wiped her mouth on her sleeve. She looked down at the abject captive, eyes jammed tight, tears streaming from the corners.

"That was okay for a first try," she told the still prone girl. "Next time, you'll do better or you'll get a red hot zap. Got it?"

Sharon did not dare to speak. She nodded her head in affirmation, her lips pursed and trembling, streaks of tears on her face.

Louise knelt down and untied the girl's ankles. Grabbing her hair, she dragged her back to the cage and ordered her in. Sharon whined and moaned as she was manhandled by the powerful woman. When she reached the cage she crawled in without hesitation. She hated being confined in the cage, but it did offer a degree of protection from the woman's assaults. The door was closed behind her and a lock affixed, securing it.

Louise wadded her panties and jammed them into the pocket of her dress. She took a long look at the pretty captive. In a few weeks she would be wearing a master's collar somewhere. She might be purchased by a private collector or she might be bought by the owners of a cathouse somewhere in the Far East or in Africa, where white flesh was rare and treasured. Whatever her ultimate destination, she represented a substantial payday for Louise and Herman. She was pretty, frail and obedient. She would make a good slave.

When Herman descended the stairs that evening, Sharon was prepared for more abuse. She preferred sucking the old man's cock to servicing Louise. Herman was quick, no nonsense. The quicker she could get him off the better.

As was his want, Herman stepped up to the cage and opened the little window. Sharon presented her head and he affixed the ring at the back of collar to the top bar. Wordlessly he presented his soft penis to the unhappy girl's mouth. The girl knew just what was required. She took the bulbous head in her mouth and started worrying it with her tongue. She had done this for Artie, her boyfriend quite a few times. According to Artie, she had gotten quite good at it. She actually liked the taste of cock and didn't mind pleasuring Artie's hard wand. He was clean, good looking and appreciative. And it was better than giving in to his insistence that they fuck. She knew that if she held out that prize, Artie might just propose. It wasn't that she was still a virgin; it was just that two of her former boyfriends had stopped seeing her soon after their conquest of her pussy. She didn't want that happening with Artie.

So Sharon knew how to enflame the old man's lust. She pulled at the cock with her lips, sucking in her breath. She could feel it rising in her mouth and at that signal, she began to bob her head backwards and forwards.

Herman appreciated the businesslike attitude of the girl. He had the prod pushed into her side in case she tried anything funny. He placed his other hand on the top of the cage to steady himself.

As the girl rubbed her lips down the length of his piece, Herman felt a quiver of pleasure flow through him. It was an energetic, well trained mouth that encircled his dick. Maybe he would have her suck off the buyer before serious negotiations began. A girl with good sucking skills was a fine asset.

It was not long before Herman felt his juices flowing. He began to counterthrust against the girl's efforts. His dick struck the back of her throat several times, making her gag. When his cock exploded, it filled her small mouth with his white, sticky jism. She had been warned about swallowing it and every drop went down her throat. Herman grunted loudly as the pleasure overcame him. He waited until the throbbing had stopped before pulling his cock free from the girl's mouth. "Now, that took the edge off," he thought to himself. Herman's policy was to try to always have at least one girl in the 'hole'. Other than pulling his own meat, it was the only sexual pleasure that he got.

Herman tucked his now flaccid cock back into his pants and zipped up. The girl had moved to the back of the cage, her eyes locked on the form of her tormentor. Herman smiled at her. "Good job, cunt," he said as he locked the small window closed. Turning from her, he crawled up the wooden ladder, unlocked the heavy, wooden door and pulled himself up and out of the dungeon. The girl shuddered as the trapdoor slammed shut behind him.

CHAPTER TWO

Maddy's Public Issues seminar let out at 8:30 every Tuesday and Thursday night. It was a long drive back to her apartment in Carlton. The Interstate took her about half way there, but the rest of the drive was along a long, curvy, two lane blacktop. She had made the drive many times. It was lonely and tiring, but her Ipod kept her entertained and it seemed to make the miles go quicker.

The stretch between Hadleysville and Newton was the worst. There were almost no stores on the road and those that were there closed at 8 P.M. or earlier. An occasional streetlight marked the few crossroads. Otherwise, the road was dark and barren.

She was about halfway through the Hadleysville-Newton stretch when her car started to shudder and cough. Her '98 Escort had been recently tuned up and she was perplexed and annoyed at the apparent problem. Suddenly, the engine cut off and Maddy coasted the car onto the small shoulder on her right. "Shit!" she spat out. "God dammit!" What could be worse than breaking down in the middle of nowhere late at night? Maddy ran the little that she knew about cars through her head. She wasn't out of gas; she had a little over a quarter of a tank. Maybe the fuel line had clogged?

She had broken up with her boyfriend, Harold, a couple of weeks ago and she didn't feel right about calling him for help. Her dad lived about an hour's drive away. A couple of her girl friends lived closer, but even if she got picked up, she would have to leave the car there, abandoned on the side of the road. That meant tomorrow she would have to deal with getting her car towed or fixed or something. "Shit! Shit! Shit!" she thought to herself.

The young girl then saw the headlights of an approaching car in her rearview mirror. She held off dialing her cell phone for help until it had passed by. "Maybe it's a cop or something," she thought. If so, she could find out where there was a local gas station open and maybe get it towed there. She had Triple A, but when she had called them in the past, it had taken hours to get towed. A local connection would be better.

It was not a cop car that was approaching behind her. The vehicle slowed down as it came near and stopped opposite her car window. It was a van, looming and somewhat ominous beside her. Maddy was about to lock the doors when the interior light in the van went on. It was a middle aged, white woman. She was pleasantly dressed and had a kindly, if homely, face. The woman lowered her passenger side window.

Seeing that the woman wanted to talk to her and hoping that she might be able to give her some helpful information, Maddy lowered the driver's window to her own car.

"What's the matter, honey?" the older woman called out. Her voice was friendly, good natured. Maddy let out a sigh of relief.

"Oh, this old heap just gave out," she replied.

"Where you headin'?" the woman asked.

"Home," Maddy replied. This woman looked okay, but you never could tell. Maddy didn't want her to know how far away from home she really was. She didn't know why, but she just had a feeling.

"You got Triple A?" the woman called over.

"Yeah, but…"

"Yeah," the woman interjected, "I know. They take ages. If you're lookin' for a tow, I got a cousin owns a small station about three miles up Route 416. He's closed now, but I could probably get him to come out and get you. He might be able to start your car for you."

Maddy weighed the woman's offer. If she agreed, and the cousin could help her out, she wouldn't have to call anyone to come get her. She wouldn't have to come back tomorrow. And she wouldn't have to sit here on the side of this deserted road, a target for any kind of maniac who happened by. The young girl looked over the older woman carefully. All she could see was the woman's expectant smile, a friendly appearance. "Oh, what the fuck," she thought.

"Yeah, thanks a lot. That would be a big help," she called out to the woman.

The woman waved at Maddy. "Come on, get in, we'll zip over to my cousin's. We'll get you back on your way home in no time."

Maddy was always being delightfully surprised at the friendliness of people in the South. She had moved here with her dad about four years ago from a Cleveland suburb. Once she graduated high school a year later, she decided to get her own place and try and make it on her own. Her dad wasn't rich and he had only moved here because all the good jobs seemed to be moving south. She liked the South. The weather was usually nice, the people were friendly and the pace of life just seemed a little slower. This woman's readiness to go out of her way was just another example of why she liked living here.

After rolling up her window, Maddy stepped out of her car and locked the door. She opened the passenger door of the van and stepped in. The driver had turned off the overheads and the rear of the van was dark. Maddy shifted a little uneasily in her chair. She turned to her rescuer. "My name's Maddy," she said.

"I know," the woman answered.

Maddy had just enough time to say, "Wha...", when a strong, rough arm circled around her throat. Her air was cut off immediately. Her eyes widened as the woman lay a length of duct tape over her mouth. Maddy started to flail with her arms at her attacker. Suddenly she received a punch to her midsection. The woman had given her a solid left hook. Maddy's body was immobilized by the blow. She desperately tried to draw in breath, but the arm around her throat blocked all oxygen. Maddy thought that she was being murdered and, as she floated into unconsciousness, she wondered why.

Herman quickly dragged the limp girl into the back of the van. Louise, after helping Herman to lift her legs over the divider between the front seats, pressed on the gas. The van pulled over to the side of the road in front of Maddy's car. By the time the van had stopped, Herman had wrist and ankle restraints on the girl. She was coming around now and pulled at her arms locked behind her back.

"Give me her keys," Herman rasped.

Louise felt along the passenger side floor and found them and Maddy's small tote bag that doubled as her pocketbook. She handed them to Herman. He opened the side door of the van, hopped out and opened the door to the Escort. He popped the hood, tossing the tote bag and the keys into the back seat of the car. He rushed around to the front, leaned over into the engine compartment and detached a small device that he had earlier attached to the gas line.

Having retrieved his little, radio operated toy, Herman slammed the hood lid down. He shut the door after relocking it. He then jumped back into the van. Louise sped off.

Maddy was still groggy, but was returning to consciousness. As the van started to move, she felt her body rolled to the side and dropped into a long, narrow compartment. Straps were tied around her legs, waist and chest. The lid to the compartment closed. Maddy was effectively shut off from the world.

"What was with the, 'I know' bullshit," Herman accosted Louise as he climbed into the passenger seat.

"Waddya mean?" she said back.

"You know what I mean!" Herman argued loudly. "She said her name and you said, 'I know'. Was that some kind of joke?"

"Oh, don't get your shorts all bunched up, Herman, what's the difference?"

"The difference is that you're not supposed to say anything more than you have to. Suppose I had to duck down because a car was coming. There'd you be sitting with your thumb up your ass trying to explain to the fucking cunt how you knew her fucking name!" Herman was as close to boiling point as he could get without actually crossing the line.

"Oh, for Christ's sake, Herman, chill out. I saw you making your move. I wanted to distract her, to surprise her."

"Just don't do it again, okay, I don't like it."

Louise went through a quick catalogue of things she didn't like about Herman but kept her mouth shut. It wasn't worth it. "Let the old goat steam," she thought.

And so for the next five hours, Herman and Louise exchanged nary a word. Herman had turned on the radio, which played a country western station. The rhythm of the road was soothing and by the time they got back to the house, they had both calmed down. It was a good thing, because there was more work to do.

Louise pulled the van up to the barn and shut off the lights. Long existing protocol was to wait in the darkness for a few minutes to make sure that no one had followed them. If someone had, there was no sense being caught carrying a protesting girl into the barn or standing there with the trap door open while police headlights shined on you. If a cop car pulled in, maybe they could talk their way out of it, or maybe Herman would have time to pull out the pump action shotgun. Fake passports and plane tickets were always kept handy when they went out on a job.

Maddy felt the van come to a halt. A million things had run through her mind as she was carted off to god knows where. She had tried to keep track of the time and the direction the van had traveled in. But it had proved to be impossible. As far as Maddy knew, they could be as far away as Georgia or Kentucky, or even Virginia. They might even still be in Tennessee. The real question was what these people were going to do to her. She waited on the next development, helpless and frightened.

When Herman and Louise were satisfied that they hadn't been followed, Louise pulled the van into the barn. Herman jumped out and closed the barn door. As Louise went to open the trap door, Herman entered the van and opened the compartment where Maddy lay. Maddy had just a moment to stare up into the dim light of the van's interior when Herman slapped two patches over her eyes. They had adhesive on their backs and they effectively blinded Maddy's sight. She gave a little cry and tried to buck herself free of her restraints. Herman availed himself of the simple expedient of holding her nose closed with his fingers. It took about ten seconds for Maddy to appreciate her vulnerability. She didn't want to lose consciousness again. She stopped struggling.

Herman untied the straps that held Maddy into the compartment and then pulled her body out. She was wearing a pair of washed out dungarees and a simple, white, cotton, short sleeved shirt. Her shoes were sneakers. Herman lifted Maddy's body by her belt and dragged her to the door of the van. He then stood her up and, pressing his shoulder into her midsection, lifted her out.

It was only about 20' between the van and the trapdoor to the 'hole'. Louise had opened it and was waiting expectantly at the bottom of the stairs. Herman carefully fed the girl's body down the ladder, headfirst. It was disconcerting for Maddy to be descending to an unknown place headfirst. It did not bode well for a prospective escape or of the intent of this couple towards her.

Finally, Maddy's body was resting on the floor of the dungeon. Herman had joined Louise there. Sharon was, of course, long gone. It had been six weeks since Maddy had first been spotted by Herman. Sharon and the girl from Jackson had been sold off three weeks ago. The Daleysville girl was lying in her cage, bound as Sharon had been, looking with fear and apprehension at the latest development in her nightmare.

The Daleysville girl, Peggy Ann, was a medium sized cheerleader type. She had a perky face, all smiles and delight. She was about 5'4' tall and was small on top. Her breast size was not really a problem since there were ways to correct that. What was a problem is that when they had snatched Peggy Ann, her friend, Maureen, had happened upon the scene. Now Maureen was a nice kid, friendly, fun to have around, but she was no beauty. She was flabby around the hips and had large, fatty thighs. Her breasts were large, mostly due to her over consumption of ice cream and potatoes. She had a stubby nose and two brown, slightly crossed eyes. She was definitely blind date material.

But since they already had Peggy Ann tied and trussed and were loading her into the van, Maureen had to go too. She gave a little cry as she perceived what was happening. Luckily, Herman had the stun gun with him and one shot put Maureen on the ground, squirming and moaning. It was a simple matter to poke the .45 in her face and secure her cooperation.

So Maureen, not really fat, but chunky, sat in the cell next to her shapely and desirable friend, Peggy Ann. They were both gagged. It was policy to gag when more than one female was imprisoned in the 'hole'. No sense in letting them plot an escape, as unlikely as that was.

Both Maureen and Peggy Ann watched wide eyed as Maddy was set down on the floor. They observed with great interest as Herman produced his long, thick Bowie knife and started cutting Maddy's clothes away. The knife sliced easily through the fabric. The shirt was off first, revealing a small lacy bra that pushed her soft orbs together and lifted them up. That lasted another two seconds as Harman cut through the straps and pulled it from her. Maddy's breasts danced free. They were pale and firm, melon sized. The nipples were stiff with fear. Maddy struggled and whimpered in protest the exposure of her treasures. She was responding purely on instinct, since it was clear even to her that she had no way to resist being stripped bare.

Herman sliced through the seam of the legs of Maddy's jeans and ripped the fabric right up to her hip. Once the belt and zipper had been undone, it was a simple matter to slice through the crotch and pull the pants off. That left Maddy lying on the dungeon floor naked except for her tiny, blue, thong panties. Her ankles were still tied together, but Herman was able to spread her knees apart and slice through the gussets. Maddy was now completely unclothed, bare, except for the tape across her mouth and the patches over her eyes.

"She's a keeper all right," Louise said as she took in the thick, but graceful form of the young girl, a Diana type. Herman was staring at her too. He yearned to put his stiff dick between those creamy thighs, feel the girl's heels digging into his back. He loved long legs. Why the hell he had ever married Louise was beyond recollection.

"Come on," Herman replied. "Let's get her into a cage. Help me stand her up."

Louise and Herman both grabbed one of Maddy's confined arms and lifted her from the floor. Maddy had heard something about a cage and her knees started to tremble. She sagged as the two captors held her in their arms. The tape was ripped from her mouth suddenly, burning her lips. Maddy took a deep breath through her mouth. She was about to begin to plead and beg for freedom when she felt a thick, leather object prod at her oral opening. Foolishly, she opened her mouth to protest and the object was jammed inside. It was a long, thick, leather plug that reached almost all the way to the back of her mouth. She tried to expel it as she felt its straps tied off behind her head.

The hands were next. Herman took his knife and placed it directly over Maddy's windpipe. Madeline felt its sharp edge and knew she was being remonstrated to keep still and cooperate. Louise unfastened the hands and applied thick leather bracelets to her wrists. Maddy felt something circle her neck and heard a 'click' as a collar was locked in place. Louise affixed a chain to one bracelet and, running it through the ringk in the collar, locked it to the other.

Herman stroked his rough hands along the girl's sides, caressing her flanks. Her skin was smooth and warm. The girl shuddered at his touch. He lifted her elbows away from her body so that he could get a better look at the delicate orbs that hung there. If Louise were not there, he would have affixed his lips to one of them. He did lay his hand under one and lift it, feeling its weight, squeezing it softly to assess its firmness. Herman was pleased by both of these exercises.

"Come on," Louise complained. "Let's get her caged up. I'm hungry."

Herman lamented his partner's presence. "Okay, okay," he answered sullenly. "Open one up."

Louise unlocked the cage next to Maureen. Maureen shied back as the woman stepped near her. Louise chuckled. "Don't worry, cunt, this time we're not here for you," she said.

With the cage door open, Herman forced Maddy to her knees, unfastened the ankle restraints and pulled her along by her hair. When she was opposite the cage door, he ripped the patches off of her eyes. Madeline was startled at his actions and it took a moment for her to accustom her eyes to the light. When she had, she saw the yawning cage before her. She had heard the couple speaking, but hardly believed what she was hearing. Now the reality was directly in front of her. She was going to be placed in a cage! She looked quickly to her right and saw the other young, naked women similarly confined. It was like some gothic horror story. She couldn't believe it. Caged women? What for?

Madeline didn't have long to contemplate that question as she felt heavy hands pushing her towards the cage door. Bound and gagged as she was, outnumbered by her two strong and determined captors, Madeline had little spirit for resistance. Choking back a sob, she crawled forwards on

her knees and entered her tiny prison. The door slammed
shut behind her and was locked.

CHAPTER THREE

Madeline watched as the man and woman who had kidnapped her wordlessly ascended the ladder and closed the trap door above. The room was filled with a deadly silence. Tears started to flow from the young girl's eyes as she realized the seriousness of her predicament. She should have gotten home long ago, washed her hair, gotten ready for bed. She could have crawled up with her cat and had a cup of tea. She would have eaten a small snack before bed, some celery with peanut butter. But what was going to happen to her now? Who were these cruel people? Would she be held for ransom, or was some other cruel purpose in mind?

The two other prisoners watched Madeline cry and empathized with her misery. They had been there a week. As of yet, their questions had remained largely unanswered. One thing they knew that Madeline did not was their captors' predilection for forced sex. Maureen did not seem suitable for sexual slavery, except for the crudest sort. So Herman had decided that she would become a permanent resident of the dungeon. She wouldn't fetch much of a price anyway. One or two more snatches and he would have all the money he would ever need. Maureen could stay behind with Louise in the hole when he closed shop.

And so Maureen had suffered the gross indignities of being raped nightly. Herman had brought down a little stool to bend her over so that he could fuck her ass. Peggy Ann watched with horror each time Maureen was dragged out of her cell, slapped into submission and fucked roundly and savagely by the large, cruel man. Sometimes he would force Peggy Ann to suck him to hardness so that he could go another bout with her heavy set friend. Sometimes he fucked Maureen to his content and then made Peggy Ann finish him off with her mouth.

Louise had tacitly consented to Herman's freedom of action as it pertained to Maureen because she saw an equal opportunity to indulge in her private delights. Maureen was crisscrossed with welts and bruises because Louise liked to whip and beat her. She would do it with the fat girl ungagged so that she could enjoy her pleas and screams. Once, she had dragged Peggy Ann from her cage and forced her to lick her strung up friend to orgasm. She then had to suck on Louise's hard clit until Louise's juices flowed over her face.

Madeline would learn of these things shortly. For now, she had enough to adjust to her new circumstances. Since she was tall and broad, the cage was a more severe confinement for her than the other girls. She barely had room to turn around in it. Sleeping would be a great difficulty, although sleep was about the farthest thing from Madeline's mind right now. She took in the abject, distorted faces of her fellow prisoners and realized that there was little hope of escape or of being released anytime soon. She had seen their faces, that of her fellow captives and of her kidnappers. This meant that she could not be released, ever. This meant that she would probably die here in this dungeon. Maddy crawled into a ball and cried.

Herman and Louise had gone back to the house and eaten their dinner. Herman was anxious to get back to the dungeon to have the new girl suck his prick. Louise was eager to have the fat girl under her lash. The two of them sat at the dinner table wordlessly, trying to figure out how they could maneuver into being first. It was Louise who broke the silence.

"I'm going to take the cunts some food. I'll be back in a little while."

Herman balked at his implied exclusion. He had been pushed around enough by this witch. "I'm going down there first and I'm going to get my cock sucked. And then I'm going to fuck the fat one. If you want to watch that's fine, but I'm not waiting until you get your own rocks off!"

Louise thought a moment. Well, why not? Maybe it would be fun to watch the old coot stick his prick in the fat girl. And she enjoyed inflicting humiliation on the good looking ones. She blamed them for their youth, their delightful bodies. Why not make the new girl suck the old man's cock in front of her? She could taunt her with it later.

"Okay," Louise drawled. "Let's go then."

The caged girls heard the trapdoor being unlocked and then saw Louise's feet descending. Maureen began to whine since she knew that this almost certainly meant another session with the whip. Peggy Ann blanched as she saw the booted feet of the old man following. This had not happened before and it portended no good.

Madeline sensed the heightened fear of her cell mates. Obviously the couple was coming down for a purpose. Her fear was justified when she saw Louise pull out a long, thin reed covered with leather. Madeline had speculated about the red stripes worn by the girl next to her. Now she knew the reason why.

Louise unlocked Maureen's cage. "Come out little piggy," she called. "Come out and play with me."

Maureen shrunk back into her cage. It was a little ritual that the two of them had. Maureen knew that she had no choice but to submit, however she would not leave the cage until Louise had brought the electric wand to bear. Louise had it now in her hand. She pushed it into the cage and pressed it against Maureen's pudgy flesh. 'Zap!' The wand emitted a fierce electric charge. Maureen jumped within her cage, screaming behind her gag. Madeline was shocked beyond all recall. She had never seen anything so cruel and callous in her life. The pain from the wand seemed excruciating. She vowed to avoid it at all costs.

Sobbing in pain, Maureen began to crawl from her tiny prison. Her bulbous breasts swayed beneath her as she leaned over to get through the tiny door.

Since Herman was there, Louise had no hesitation in unlocking Maureen's hands. Up to now, she had kept them locked so that the girl could not strike out at her. She had merely affixed the ring in the front of the collar to a chain that she had hung from a hook in the ceiling. Today, she would raise Maureen's hands above her head. She wanted to whip her tits, something she had been unable to do before.

Maureen sniveled and whined as her hands were unlocked from her collar and affixed to the chain from the ceiling. Louise stood on a stool and raised the chain up. The ceiling was about ten feet high and so there was plenty of room to stretch the girl out her entire length.

Herman watched his wife attend to the fat girl admiringly. The old cow still had some life left in her. Too bad she wasn't twenty years younger. But this would be a show he would enjoy.

Louise rubbed Maureen's breasts with her hands, licking the nipples and squeezing them hard. She ran her hand down the girl's protruding stomach and grabbed at her snatch. She pulled sharply on the hairs that covered her sex. Maureen protested and tried to pull her hips away from the old lady. Louise merely pursued Maureen's cunt with her hand and, having gotten purchase on the twin lips that bracketed her juicy hole, pressed them together, vise-like. Maureen's eyes squinted with the pain, tears running out of the corners. She moaned loudly. Louise just smiled. "Just getting started, dearie," she said. "A little warm up. Tonight I'm going to whip your big fat tits until you scream your throat hoarse. Then Herman here is going to fuck that big broad ass of yours. Okay?"

Maureen's expression indicated that it was not okay. But her permission was not really needed.

Louise loosened Maureen's gag and pulled it from her mouth. Maureen immediately began to beg and cry.

"Oh, please, lady, please, don't whip my tits, please! I couldn't stand it! Please, I'll do anything! Please!"

Louise ignored the girl's ranting. She stepped back and swung the leather reed with all of her might. 'Smack!' It landed across both of Maureen's breasts, just above the fat, thick nipples. Maureen screamed in pain.

"Ahhhhhhhhhhhh!" she cried. She tried to twist and turn her body so that her breasts were not accessible to Louise's whip. Louise just smiled and, taking two small ropes from a wall mounted closet, knelt and tied Maureen's ankles to the rings in the floor, about four feet apart. This had the effect of stretching Maureen's body, causing her breasts to jut out prominently.

"Now, sweetie," she said, "we can begin in earnest. I want to strike every inch of those big boobies of yours."

Maureen resumed her pleas. Undeterred, Louise swung the reed back again and brought it forwards with a loud 'whoosh!' This blow struck just under Maureen's nipples. She screeched again in pain, straining at her confinements.

"Nooooooo! Ahhhhhhhhhhh!"

Louise was in near ecstasy. Her eyes were on fire, her face red with passion. Again she struck Maureen's breasts. And again. Maureen's howls were now continuous. Her words were unintelligible.

Herman was taking all of this in with untrammeled delight. His cock was hard as a stone and ached for attention. His eyes were pinned on the flabby globes of the girl's ass as she danced and gyrated in response to her whipping. Finally, Herman could take no more. He pulled his pants down and shucked them off. He took off his red and black checked, flannel shirt. It was a long time since he was naked in front of Louise, but he didn't give a shit. He was going to fuck that ass no matter what.

Seeing Herman stripped naked, Louise gave out a laugh. "Come and get it Herman!" she yelled. "Fuck this bitch silly!"

Herman stepped up behind Maureen and parted her ass cheeks. He saw the brown star between them and shot a wad of spit onto it for lubrication. Maureen was sobbing, decrying her abuse and humiliation. "Why don't they do this to Peggy Ann or the new girl?" she thought miserably. "Why are they torturing me?"

Herman pressed the bulb of his cock's head into Maureen's private place. She stiffened as she felt it. He had fucked her there before, but not while the big lady watched, enjoying her abasement. And not standing up, stretched out for all to see.

Maureen cried in pain as Herman shoved his meat past the narrow entrance. He reveled in pleasure as the tight ring slid over his shaft. He began to pump in earnest, bringing a fresh cascade of tears and wails from the girl as he pushed his cock home.

Meanwhile, Louise determined to recommence the girl's whipping. Herman's hands were around her waist as he held her steady, the better to pierce her. Her tits were still free and not yet marked to Louise's satisfaction. 'Crack!' Another blow landed on Maureen's abused mounds. She had been preoccupied by Herman's assault on her rear portal and was taken by surprise by the sudden blast of pain. She barely had time to breath in, prefatory to a piteous scream, when another blow landed, taking her breath away. Louise methodically covered the breasts with the red leavings of her whip. Maureen bucked and brayed as she was overwhelmed by painful and humiliating sensations. She wanted to expel the invader in her rear and to grab the hand that was whipping her and compel it to stop. Both of these were impossible, and so she was forced to continue to suffer the insufferable.

Herman slammed his thighs against the girl's ass again and again. He could feel the imminent explosion of his cock. He leaned his head back and groaned mightily. Suddenly, his whole body jerked and shuddered with pleasure. Load after load of his sperm was jetted into the fat girl's bowels. Finally, with one loud, long groan, he shot his last load and came to rest, his knees weak and sagging, holding onto the fat girl's body for support.

Louise's passion was on the boil. She needed her cunt licked now. She opened Peggy Ann's cage and pulled her out by the hair. She undid her gag and, sitting on the stool, spread her legs wide. She raised her skirt and the frightened Peggy Ann looked up at her. There was a notable lack of underclothes. "Lick my slit, you stupid cunt," she said. Peggy Ann knew what she had to do, and as Louise raised the hem of her skirt, Peggy Ann crept underneath it. She felt her way to the apex of Louise's thighs and found the moist, musky sex. She extended her tongue its length and began to lick the old woman's gash. The woman's hairy bush pressed against her face as she delved deeply into the hot canal. Slowly bringing her tongue upwards, she located the hard button of pleasure and sucked on it hard.

Louise was panting heavily, overcome with lust. She pulled her skirts higher and grabbed the head that pleasured her, pressing it further into her loins.

"Yes! Yes! Yes, you cunt!" she cried. Her face was flush with excitement, her eyes closed. Herman had not seen this kind of passion from the old girl in ten years. He wondered what he had been missing. But why fuck that old wrinkled cunt when he had this young, fresh pussy? He had his hand in Maureen's quim and was stroking the girl to unwelcomed pleasure. Maureen was shocked at her own feelings of lust. She had been treated more cruelly than she had ever imagined she would be, had suffered pain more excruciating than she thought possible. Yet her pussy was dripping with the evidence of her arousal. Her ass still stung from its invasion, but even that had stoked her passion. She began to utter small cries of pleasure as she tried to resist the inevitable. Her cries were mingled with that of Louise who was just about to crest into a powerful orgasm.

The two women came almost simultaneously. The small dungeon echoed with their cries of pleasure.

As Maureen's orgasm subsided and her voice lowered to tiny sighs, Herman stroked his resuscitated cock. It was thick with the mixture of the fruits of Maureen's ass and his own juices. Not wanting to get any of his charges sick, something that might detract from their selling price, he turned on the hose that Louise used to wash down the girls and, using some soap, cleaned his softened cock. When he was done, he turned towards the new girl.

Madeline had been overwhelmed by the spectacle of Maureen's torture and abuse. She had been amazed to watch the orgasms of Maureen and Louise. Seeing the old man turn to her, she knew that it would now be her turn to supply pleasure to this man's cock. She cringed in her cage as he approached her. She whined as he opened it and, prodding her with the electric wand, motioned for her to get out. She started to sob as the man released her gag and grabbed her by the hair. Kneeling before him, his hardening cock poised at her mouth, Madeline contemplated resistance. She knew that she would suffer the bite of the electric wand. She could withstand one, maybe two shocks. But not three or four. Ultimately she would succumb. The weeping girl surrendered to the inevitable.

Madeline opened her mouth to receive her captor's dick. He slid it slowly between her lips. Her stomach turned at the thought of where it had recently been. Hesitatingly, she touched the cock with her tongue. Herman was growing impatient.

"Suck my cock, you worthless whore!" he called out to her, fastening his fist harder in her hair. "Take it in your mouth and suck my come down your throat!"

Maddy, frightened beyond rationality, complied eagerly with the man's demands. "Just do it! Just do it!" she recited to herself. Her lips were pursed around Herman's shaft as he plunged his cock in and out of her mouth. She washed the tip and shaft with her tongue. Being his second orgasm in a short while, this one would be a little longer in coming. Madeline worked hard to accelerate the man's climax. He groaned with pleasure as he assaulted her mouth with his cock, ramming up against her throat. When he came, he flooded her oral cavity with his salty fluids. Madeline struggled to swallow it all, yet small drops escaped the corners of her mouth. Herman's body stiffened as he poured his juices into the girl. When he was finished, he withdrew slowly. He saw the drops of sperm that were dripping from the corners of Madeline's mouth. He looked over and saw Louise and Peggy Ann watching. He motioned to the collared woman to crawl over.

"Lick my come from this slut's face, whore. And then kiss her with your mouth open, lick her spermy tongue!"

Peggy Ann crawled over to the tearful Madeline and licked the white drippings from the corners of her mouth. Unhesitatingly, she forced her mouth on Madeline's and pressed her tongue inside. Madeline was overwhelmed by the smell of Louise's musky discharges on Peggy Ann's face. But she held her place, returning the kiss. Surprisingly, she felt her cunt warm as Peggy Ann's tongue danced with hers in her mouth. But, since their tormentors had been sated, the kissing girls were soon separated, regagged and forced back into their cells.

"I'll be back to feed and wash you, cunts," Louise told them. Maureen was left hanging from her chain. Her gag was reaffixed.

All three girls watched the legs of their abusers ascend the ladder and disappear from view. Then they all broke down and cried.

CHAPTER FOUR

Sheriff John Peabody was on the telephone in his office. He was not a happy man. It was the third time this week he had spoken to this particular caller and he had just about had it. But protocol required him to stay calm.

"No, Mr. Burnham, we don't have anything new.........Yes, we're putting all our available men on it.........No, we don't have any suspects....... Yes, we'll keep on the case......."

The Sheriff slammed the phone back into the receiver. "That dick headed, pointy toed, New York, cocksuckin' sonofabitch!" he yelled. Dotty, his secretary, cringed at the foul words. She opened a little notebook she kept and wrote it down. She had read an article about hostile workplace environments and figured pretty soon that she'd have enough for her lawsuit.

The Sheriff tried to calm himself. He had been Sheriff of Carter County for the last seventeen years. He had been a member of the Department for over thirty. Nobody was going to tell him how to run an investigation. For all he knew the girl had run off with somebody. Yes, there was the fact that her car was abandoned in the middle of nowhere. And there was the fact that her tote bag and her keys were found in the car. And yes, she hadn't told anyone she was going anywhere. But to say he was doing nothing, well that was a load of shit!

"Goddam, mother fucking Yankee," he brawled out. Dotty reached for her notebook.

In New York, in his penthouse office, Michael Burnham, President of Burnham Industries, was fit to be tied. "That goddam, incompetent, lazy, ignorant, stupid, fucking cracker!" he yelled as the phone sailed across the room. It struck the finely decorated executive wall with a clatter and the plastic broke into about twenty different pieces.

Sitting in front of Mr. Burnham's desk was Liz, his executive secretary and Paul, his administrative assistant. Paul made a little note on his pad, "New phone for Mr. Burnham."

Burnham looked up. He felt better. He always did when he smashed something. He looked at the wall. "Damn," he thought, "the new wallpaper."

Burnham was not the kind of man who took the disappearance of his niece lightly. Madeline was his shiftless brother's only child, and he had none. He had offered many times to get her out of that one horse town where she lived and set her up at the college of her choice. Being number 73 on the Fortune 500 'Richest Men in America' list, he had pull just about everywhere. But no, she loved the South, she wanted to make it on her own. "Fuck!" Burnham shouted.

"Okay," he thought. Time to quit fucking around. "Get me Barnes!" he ordered.

* * * * * * * * * * *

Jacob Barnes was easing himself into a very willing, moist, hot cunt. He had felt like an afternoon fuck and had called Jackie, his favorite, local call girl. He and Jackie went back a ways. He had helped her out of a big jam. She fucked him for free.

"Come on baby!" she called out. "Give it to me, come on, give it to me!" Beads of perspiration hung on her shiny, coffee colored skin. She had long, muscular legs and they were wrapping themselves around Jacob's waist. He groaned as his cock pressed past the distended, flush lips of Jackie's pussy. He loved to fuck Jackie. She loved to fuck.

"Ohhhhhhh, baby!" she yelled as she felt the hot member delve into her yearning gash. "Oh, give it to me!"

Jacob, Jake to his friends and acquaintances, was humping the tall, beautiful black girl madly. Twenty minutes of fellatio and cunnilingus had primed his pump. He felt his cock explode at the same moment that his cell phone began to ring.

"Oh, fuck!" he yelled. He wasn't always vocal when he came, but Jackie brought this out in him. "Yeah! Yeah! Yeah!" he shouted as he jetted a stream of cum inside the wriggling girl.

She felt his orgasm, felt his body tighten, felt the warmth of his discharge and she was off too. "Oh, fuck me! Fuck me! Fuck me!" she yelled as she pushed her hips into Jake's, clutching at his broad naked back.

By the time the two backed monster stopped its writhing gyrations, the telephone had long stopped ringing. Jake lay as limp as a sock on washing day. His heart was pounding madly in his chest. Jackie was cooing and smiling underneath him.

"Oh, Jake," she intoned, "what you do to me."

"Likewise honey," Jake returned. "Likewise."

Jackie looked at the small pink plastic watch on her wrist. "Oh, baby, I've got a date. I've got to get going."

"Sure, honey," Jake whispered. He admired her stamina. He slid his body off of hers and lay next to her in the king sized, plush, four star hotel bed. When Jake fucked, he liked to do it right. Besides, Jackie deserved the best treatment.

"I'm going to shower quick, baby," Jackie said as she threw her legs over the side of the bed. She stood about 6' tall in her bare feet. She had wide hips and large, pillowy breasts. She had tight, sculpted muscles where it counted, and she was a first class whore.

As Jackie scurried to the bathroom, Jake pulled out his cell phone and checked his caller i.d. It was his service. There were only about ten or fifteen people in the world that had Jake's cell phone number. He had a program installed that blocked his i.d. on all outgoing calls. He speed dialed his service.

Jake didn't believe in voice mail. Voicemail didn't screen out the bullshit. And voicemail just lay there waiting to be retrieved. He had trained his service well. They knew what calls were important and they would keep calling every twenty minutes or so until they got him.

A flat sounding, female voice answered. "Messages," she said.

"This is Mr. Green. You called me."

"Yes, Mr. Green," the voice continued. Please call 212-555-2465 as soon as possible."

That meant that the call had come in from one of his "hot" numbers, a list of important callers he had given to his service.

"Thank you," he said and hung up.

A few moments later he was on the phone with Burnham.

"Jake, I need you. When can you be in New York?"

Jake was in Chicago, the home of blues and great jazz. He played a mean saxophone and, when he wasn't working, he liked to get a gig with some of the boys and jam. On the music circuit he was known as Billy Boggs. He had other names too.

"I can be there in three hours." Jake knew that if Burnham was calling there was a real emergency. And as for payment, that would not be a problem.

"Okay, I'll have a packet sent out to you now. Tell my secretary where you are, if you can."

"No problem, Mr. Burnham," Jake responded. "I'll have a preliminary plan by the time I get there. This is a no holds barred matter?"

"Absolutely!" Burnham answered emphatically.

"See you around four o'clock your time." Jake rang off. He speed dialed Burnham's secretary. She emailed a set of documents to a confidential employee at Burnham's Chicago office who messengered it to Mr. Green at Jake's hotel.

By the time Jake got to New York, he was up to speed on the problem. He had made a few calls. Leon and Curley were booked, but might be available in a couple of days. Tucker, Martinez and his tech guy, Irving Ostroff, would all be in New York at 7 P.M.

At 6 A.M. the next day, Jake and his team landed at Carter County Airport. A rented, silver Lexus awaited them there. The drive to the County Administration Building was short, about 20 minutes. They were at Sheriff Peabody's office at 6:30.

Peabody had told Burnham to go fuck himself when he was told that Burnham wanted to send in his own team. Fifteen minutes later a telephone call from the Governor's office convinced him otherwise. The Sheriff was there at 6:30 along with his chief of investigations.

"Good morning, Sheriff," Jake said. He introduced his team, first names only. "I'd like to look over your reports. Please give Irving here a list of evidence you've found and then let him take a look at it. I want to speak to the responding officer."

"The what?" the Sheriff asked.

"First officer on the scene." You numbskull, Jake thought.

"Sure," the Sheriff answered. "That'd be Corporal Johnson. He's off duty now, but he comes on at 10."

Jake gave the Sheriff a cold look. "I'd like to see him at 7:30."

The Sheriff gave Jake a dirty look. Then he remembered the Governor. The Sheriff was up for reelection. "7:30, okay," he said.

Jake sat in a conference room with Tucker and Martinez. They had all read the reports. There were some interviews with Maddy's classmates, her professor, a few friends, some guys at the bar and, of course, Harold, the former boyfriend.

"As I see it" Tucker said, "we've got to eliminate the boyfriend first."

"Right," Jake said. "I'm going to get a full write up on everyone in the girl's class. Martinez, I want you to stake out the parking lot at the college for a few days. If we've got a serial killer, he might come back to trawl for more."

"Sure Jake," Martinez answered.

"What have you got?" Jake asked Irving.

Irving replied. "Not much. They didn't do the girl's tires, it rained the next morning, they had the car towed without getting prints, and they searched it without any quarantine measures, so that they probable shed all kinds of things in the car passenger compartment."

"Great," Jake deadpanned.

"They have her tote bag and her keys. That's about it."

"Anything off of them?

"Yeah," Irving answered. "There we may have got lucky. The bag was found in the back seat. Now if I was a college girl coming home from class, I'd have the bag on the front seat next to me. More importantly, her Ipod is still in it. There's a small stain of mud or clay on the bottom of the outside of the bag. Not something I'd expect from a girl who was as clean as this girl was, based on the rest of the car. I think that somehow the bag got out of the car. Maybe she was going somewhere and took it with her. Then the guy who snatched her threw it back into the car. And maybe he got some mud on it first. I'll have some scrapings up to the lab by this afternoon. We should have a report tomorrow."

"Good. Go take a look at the scene. I know it's been a week, but there might be something out there that the rain didn't wash away and the stumblebums missed."

"Okay. I'm going to have the car vacuumed and dusted anyway. Who knows?"

"Fine. I'm going out to the girl's apartment. It's been gone over once, but I want to see it for myself. There's always the chance the Sheriff is right and the girl ran off with someone. It's doubtful, but we need to exclude it for sure."

The men broke up without further ado.

* * * * * * * * * * *

Herman pulled his dick from Madeline's mouth. A line of cum dribbled over her lip. She licked it in. She had been taught. Although she had vowed to do everything that she could to avoid the fierce bite of the electric wand, it was Herman's policy to make sure all the girl's got a taste of it. Maddy had been right, after the third one, she was willing to do anything he or Louise wanted.

Maddy had become Herman's favorite. She looked all forlorn and pitiful scrunched up in her tiny cage. He liked to watch her eyes fill up with tears as she pleasured his stiff prick. She was good at it too. Probably had some experience.

Maddy had had some experience. She had been a little wild before she moved to Carter County with her dad. Blow jobs were the staple of Jefferson High student sex life. No one wanted to get 'preggers'. And it kept the boys content. Besides, she liked it.

Harold, her local boyfriend, had been startled the first time she placed her lips on his tool. He was a mild mannered country boy, just the opposite of what Maddy had known in Cleveland. But he got used to it real fast. She had finally convinced him to reciprocate just before they broke up. Maddy wasn't completely sure that that wasn't the reason.

But sucking this fat man's wad was nothing like sucking a muscle-bound halfback's tool in the front seat of a Mustang convertible. He smelled, and he pulled and pinched her tits while she worked on his rod. He was crude and he held that three foot long wand in his hand the entire time.

Herman had left after his morning bj and Maddy knelt regagged in her small prison. The old lady would be by soon with their food and to clean their wastes. She made Maddy present her rear to her so that she could wipe and apply lotion to her twin portals. She would kneel with her head to the bottom of the cage, her ass hanging out of the cage's door. The old witch got off on bringing Maddy to the edge of orgasm. Maddy would be panting and swaying her ass, unable to resist the expert manipulation of her tender canal and its button of pleasure. Just as she approached her crises, the woman would stop and laugh. She would then slap her ass and tell her to "pull it in". Maddy would draw her rear end back into the cage so that the woman could lock her back up. Then she would do the same thing to the other girls. Only once had the old lady gone too far. Maddy had begun to shake and quiver as she felt the pulses of pleasure run through her. The old lady had gotten mad and shoved her ass back into the cage with her foot. Maddy just lay there letting the echoes of her orgasm subside. That was when she got one of the jolts from the wand. After that, she knew better and held her orgasm back with all of her might.

When she was done cleaning the girls' pussies and asses, the old lady would pour their wastes into a bucket and wash out with a hose the pans into which they shitted and pissed. There was a drain in the middle of the floor that apparently led to a pump somewhere. After replacing the pans, the old lady would place a fixture on the hose that injected soap into the flow. She would then hose the girls down, covering them with cold, soapy water. After rinsing them off, she would drop some disinfectant on the floor and then leave.

At least once a day, she would come back and torture Maureen, the fat girl. She was a little thinner now. She would scream and plea for mercy as she was beaten. Her tits were crosshatched with lacerations as was her ass. Herman would often watch and then fuck her up the ass standing there, or in the pussy while bent over the stool.

Peggy Ann seemed to have been forgotten by the pair of cruel kidnappers. That was all right with her.

On the sixth day of Maddy's captivity, they brought another girl down into the 'hole'. She was a tiny blonde thing. Her hair was long and wispy, almost like gossamer. She had a thin but shapely frame, blue eyes and a pretty face. She moaned and whined almost constantly in her cage. Maddy wanted to kick her to get her to shut up, but the bars of the cage prevented her. She felt guilty, but took a small amount of satisfaction when she saw the girl zapped several times. That didn't shut her up though.

On the eighth day, there was a change in routine. It was late in the afternoon. There had been an ominous lack of activity. No morning blow job, no hosing down. No food. The light was always on in the dungeon, but when the trapdoor opened the girls could see whether it was day or night by the quality of the light that filtered in. Maddy didn't know it was the afternoon, of course, only that her last meal had been a long time ago.

When Louise and Herman came down the steps of the ladder, they carried hoods and a bag of soaps and lotions. Peggy Ann was first. Louise dragged her out of the cage and had her kneel in the middle of the room. She took the hose with the soap attachment and shoved it up Peggy Ann's rectum. Peggy Ann was greatly discomforted by this new development, but she remained silent. She felt her stomach distend and a queasy liquidity in her bowels. Louise took the hose away and slapped Peggy Ann's ass. "Okay, out with it shit for brains," she said caustically. Peggy Ann was directly over the drain and she let loose a gush of brown stained water. Louise repeated the process and Peggy Ann reciprocated. Louise ran the hose over her ass and over the floor, washing the wastewater down the drain.

Standing the girl up, her hands folded under her neck in an attitude of prayer, Louise hosed her down. She augmented the soapy water by scrubbing her body with an oversized sponge. She scoured the girl thoroughly and washed her hair. For the first time in days, Peggy Ann's long brown hair was washed and brushed. She cried and complained through her gag as the brush ruthlessly detangled her rat's nest. All the while, Herman stood watching. He was enjoying the show.

When Louise was finished, she had Peggy Ann crouch over the drain and pee, wiping her afterwards. Herman affixed a leash to Peggy Ann's collar and unlocked her wrists. He then led her up the ladder. Peggy Ann had a little trouble negotiating the rungs as her legs hadn't gotten much use for almost three weeks. But she was eager to leave the dungeon no matter what fate awaited her upstairs. With Louise pushing her ass from underneath, she was able to mount the ladder and disappeared from view.

Louise did the blonde girl next. When she was up the stairs, it was Maddy's turn.

Maddy submitted to the cleansing with trepidation. Although she enjoyed the prospect of being really clean for the first time in a week, she knew that whatever the purpose had been in kidnapping her, she would find out what it was once she had left the 'hole'. She had been blindfolded when brought down and so had no idea what was up there. The fact that the other two girls, Maddy, of course had no idea what their names were, had not been blindfolded when brought up meant that their captors didn't care what they saw. Maddy wasn't sure what that meant, but was sure it wasn't good.

When she had peed in the drain, Maddy allowed herself to be guided up the stairs. She reached the top and saw that they were in a tired, old barn. Herman held her leash and the wand. She thought momentarily of attempting an escape. But as soon as she breached the top of the stairs and crawled onto the barn floor, Herman affixed a set of hobbles on her ankles. She couldn't get far in them.

What Madeline saw as she was pulled to her feet startled her. The blond and the brunette were standing in the middle of the barn. Behind each of them was a wooden frame. Each frame had a wooden arm that extended forwards from the top. A steel bar was affixed horizontally to the top, perpendicular to the wooden arm. On each side of the bar there were chains that descended to the ends of a wooden yoke. The girls were standing there, their necks and hands locked into the yokes, as if on display. There were black bags over their heads. The skinny blond girl was whimpering as usual.

Maddy was dragged over to the third frame. She didn't want to be displayed. Her hands were free and she tugged on the leash that Herman held. The thick limbed, heavy set man had no problem drawing her towards him. Holding the leash with one hand he placed the electric wand between Maddy's legs. He gave her a jolt; she collapsed, screaming. If not for the chain which held her head and neck up, Maddy would have fallen to the floor. Choking, she regained her feet as soon as she could. She looked with fear into the smiling man's face. He held the wand poised at her sex. Her gag had been removed when she was cleaned and she was able to croak out a desperate plea, "No, please, I'll behave, please."

"Then cut the shit," Herman snarled. "Get over here!" he commanded.

Madeline allowed Herman to remove her bracelets and then place her hands and neck in the yoke. The yoke passed just above her collar and held her head high. Since she was taller than the other girls, Herman adjusted the chains that held up either end of the yoke so that Maddy's body was fully extended. Herman stood back and admired her. She was a little taller than him, even barefoot. Herman congratulated himself. She was just what the doctor ordered. He caressed her breast, squeezing the nipple until Maddy grimaced. He laughed.

Herman took a black rubber ball from his pocket. It was about the size of a Spaldeen, maybe just a little bit smaller. "Open your mouth," he commanded. Maddy complied meekly. The ball was pushed in, distending her mouth and effectively silencing her. Pulling a black cloth bag from his pocket he placed it over her head and drew the string.

Maddy was now effectively blinded and gagged. The nakedness of her body, exposed below the yoke, was somehow intensified by the hood that covered her head. It was if there were two parts of her. Her head and hands, the parts that expressed her humanity and her individuality, above the yoke, were imprisoned and confined. The other part, bearing the objects of men's lusts, was free below, free to the hands of anyone who cared to touch her.

Maddy felt the man release her ankles from the hobble. Her feet were then pulled apart and something attached, first to one ankle and then the next. It was a three foot long bar. Her legs were now spread wide, the lips of her sex parted and exposed. Since she had been pulled almost to her full height by the yoke after Herman adjusted it, Maddy felt the pressure of the yoke on her neck as it pressed on her chin. She had to stand on her tip toes to avoid choking. Herman noted her discomfiture and adjusted the chains to the yoke slightly. It was better, but Maddy was still extended and stretched out almost as far as she could go. It didn't take long for her to feel the cramps in her feet and calves as she arched her feet to relieve pressure on her neck.

Down in the hole, Maureen awaited her turn at being washed and removed from the dungeon. She was surprised when she saw Louise packing up the sponges and brushes and putting the hose away. Louise looked over at her, a gleam in her eyes. "You're not going anywhere, little piglet. You're staying here so we can have more fun."

Maureen moaned in despair. She tried to plead with the woman to let her go with her friend and the others. Her words came out mumbled and distorted by her gag. Louise paid no mind as she finished cleaning up. She ascended the steps and closed the door. Maureen heard the door slam as if it was a death sentence.

CHAPTER FIVE

It was about four o'clock in the afternoon now. Jake had examined Maddy's apartment without gaining any insights as to her whereabouts. One thing he had learned was that it was unlikely that Maddy had run off without telling anyone. Her rooms were neat as a pin. Everything was in its place. She had left behind a diary that gave no hint that she was embroiled in a secret love affair. There was food in the refrigerator for several days. Mail had accumulated, but there was nothing there of interest.

Jake sat in the Sheriff's conference room and received reports from Tucker and Irving.

"I checked the scene, Jake, and there's nothing there," Irving informed him. "No skid marks, no debris on the shoulder, nothing. I've vacuumed the car and sent it and the mud from the tote bag to Tallahassee. I told them to work on it overnight. We'll have prelims in the morning."

Jake looked over at Tucker. Tucker had gone to see the boyfriend. He had spent a couple hours with him. Although no worse for wear, Tucker did push him to the limits of his tolerance for pain. If he wasn't telling the truth, Tucker would jump off a bridge.

"No dice on the boyfriend," he told Jake. He was a man of few words.

Although he hadn't expected the solution to Madeline's disappearance to roll off a shelf, Jake had hoped for more than this.

"Okay," he said. "I think we can all agree that she's been snatched. By who and what for, we don't know. I'm going to connect with my FBI contact and see if there's anything by way of a suspected serial killer in the area. Jim," he was speaking to Tucker, "I want you to spell Martinez. Tell him that after a dinner break he should come back and the two of you stake the place out. It's a long shot but if it hits it'll be a home run."

"Yeah, Jake," Tucker replied. He had been on many jobs with Jake. He was older than Jake, in his early fifties. He was tall, about 6'4" and broad shouldered. His close cropped, grey hair covered an almost block shaped head, his square jaw conveyed his intense sense of purpose, as Harold had discovered.

Jake was small, about 5'7". His hair was brown, also cut short, but long enough to flow past the tops of his ears and to force him to give a boyish swipe of his hand when it fell across his forehead and into his eyes. His eyes were a light grey, as neutral as his regular demeanor. He had strong hands, large for his arms, but was not ham-fisted. He was tautly muscled. His posture always suggested the chance that he would leap out of his chair and into action. He walked with a gentle grace, cat like. He was an efficient team leader, had killed before, many times, and usually got whatever he was after, whether that was a hostage in the jungles of Colombia, a stolen shipment of gold, or, as in this case, a missing beauty.

Burnham had given him a couple of pictures back in New York and he had found more in the girl's apartment. Jake had a connoisseur's eye for female flesh, his only true weakness. He had admired the delicious curves of Maddy's body. One of the pictures had been taken in the summer at a lake, and she was wearing a small two piece. Her eyes were delightful, containing a liveliness that he was sure would be even more intense in person. There was something haunting about her. He was going to be really pissed if someone had killed her. He put the picture in his herringbone jacket pocket.

Irving looked just as you'd expect a tech nerd to look. He had short, curly, black hair, stood no more than 5'6", wore a cotton, plaid, short sleeved, dress shirt with a pocket in the front that always carried a felt tip pen. But he knew his stuff and had worked with Jake often. He had access to the best labs in the world and seldom missed a thing.

"Ah, Jake" he said, "there was one more thing."

"Yeah?" Jake replied.

"When I took a look at the car, there was nothing wrong with it. It started right up and ran for twenty minutes no problem."

"And?" Jake asked.

"And if the car broke down from a malfunction, that would be one thing. The other alternative, assuming that this was a snatch, was that the car was forced off the road. But there were no skid marks, if the police reports can be trusted, and no damage to the car."

"Okay," Jake urged his specialist on.

"Well, I have to assume that the car was either stopped voluntarily or it broke down. If we're ruling out a runaway scenario, it must have broken down. But it was working fine. So I took a look under the hood. Everything seemed normal until I looked at the gas line. There was a small imprint on the rubber hose, like it had been clamped."

"Clamped?"

"Yeah, clamped. In the glove compartment, there was a receipt from a local garage, the one across from the bar where she worked. She had a tune up and the oil changed the week before her disappearance. No mention of hoses. We should check it out."

"Well, let's say that the mechanic tells us that he didn't clamp the hose, what does that say to us?" Jake asked.

Irving leaned over in his seat as if to give special emphasis to his words. "If I was going to stop a car without forcing it off of the road, and I had access to the car beforehand, I'd rig a little radio signal doohickey that would press a clamp on the gas line. The car can't run without gas."

"That means that this is a probably a professional job." Jake observed.

"Correctamundo, Senor Jake." Irving was always pleased with himself when he pulled gold from lead. "Or a very smart amateur," he added. "My guess would be on the former."

Jake broke up the meeting. He would check out the mechanic. He told Irving to design a prototype of what he would need and then list the parts. They might get lucky and find something that was esoteric enough that they could track it to a few sales locations. Better yet, maybe mail order.

"I'll have it for you in the morning," the tech man promised.

* * * * * * * * * * *

The three naked prisoners spent a very uncomfortable couple of hours, standing, legs splayed, their heads and arms imprisoned. The bags over their heads made their breath intake stale as the air they breathed out was recirculated. It took a deep breath to get a good charge of oxygen. The lack of substantial oxygen made them groggy.

Louise had removed the bags momentarily so that she could apply some eyeliner and makeup to the girl's faces. Each of them wore a coat of bright red lipstick, rouged cheeks and dark lines around their eyes. After the bags were replaced, she rouged their nipples too.

It was about 7:30 that night that a dirty, brown delivery van rolled slowly up the gravel driveway. The truck's headlights bounced jerkily over the house as the truck maneuvered through the potholed pathway. Herman was sitting on the porch, drinking a Stroh's and smoking a Camel. The guy was late. He hated that. But the arrival of the van meant a payday. He rose to greet the driver and passenger.

Louise had stayed in the barn to mind the girls. The chances of them slipping their bonds was slim, but it didn't hurt to be careful. They couldn't get far very fast with their legs in the spreader bars, but it would be hard to explain a stiff legged, naked girl emerging from the woods and flagging down a car.

The two men stepped out of the van after maneuvering it so that the rear was facing the garage. They were dressed like delivery guys, light brown uniforms, little brown baseball caps. The truck said Nationwide Uniforms on it in large, gold letters. It carried an address in Elizabeth, New Jersey.

The driver was tall and thin, thirtyish. The other guy was shorter and stockier. He was younger, early twenties. Herman walked up to the men and shook their hands.

"Glad to see ya," he said.

"Sure," the tall one said.

"Can I get you anything, a beer or something?" Herman asked ingratiatingly.

The young guy looked like he was going to say 'yes', when the tall guy said, "Thanks, no. We've got a lot of driving to do tonight. Coffee before we go maybe."

"No problem," Herman answered. "Well, you want to see the goods?" he continued.

"That's what we're here for," the tall one said.

Herman led the men to the barn. He opened the tall, broad door and a slanting ray of light fell outside. The men entered and he closed the door behind them.

The three black hooded girls were standing directly under the only light in the place. Louise had covered the windows with sack cloth so the men could expect privacy. You can't be too careful. The tall man took charge. "Let me see the big girl first," he said.

"Sure, help yourself," Herman replied.

The two men approached Maddy. The tall man looked appreciatively over her exposed flesh. "Nice," he said. "Just like the picture." He stepped up and, using both hands, weighed her large, firm, round breasts.

Maddy had heard the door to the barn open and several sets of feet enter. It was funny how you could hear better when your sight was obscured, especially if it had been for a long time. She heard the complimentary words of the stranger. While she had been immobilized, made up and cleaned up, Maddy had concluded the unimaginable. She was going to be sold to somebody. Somebody who liked pretty girls. Somebody who would undoubtedly fuck her and use her. The sensation of the man measuring her breasts confirmed her fears.

The tall guy ran his hands down Maddy's legs. From a crouched position, he pulled out a tape measure. He looked up at Herman. "Do you mind?" he asked.

"No, no, go right ahead," Herman answered.

The man took the tape measure and ran it the length of the inside of Maddy's thigh. He seemed to be pleased. He then measured the circumference of her thighs and the broadness of her hips. He ran the tape around her back and measured her bust size. "38," he said to himself.

Rising, he spoke again to Herman. Louise was hovering by Herman's side watching the buyer taking stock of the goods. "Let me see her face."

Louise stepped forward and withdrew the hood. Maddy's eyes blinked at the sudden infusion of light. Once adjusted, they widened at the harsh, businesslike face of the man who was assessing her. "Spit out the ball," he said to her.

Maddy was so frightened that she almost peed right there. She saw Herman standing by, the electric wand now in his hand. She would obey.

With some difficulty, Madeline pushed the ball out of her mouth with her tongue. It landed on the man's palm, covered with the moisture of her mouth. The man flipped it to Herman nonchalantly.

He pressed wide Maddy's cheeks to examine her teeth. He pushed her head side to side, looking for blemishes. He stared into her eyes, assessing the spirit of the female displayed before him. He could tell a lot about a girl by looking into her eyes, especially a frightened one. He had been at this for some time.

The man removed a picture from his pocket and examined it beside Maddy's face. It was the same girl all right. One more thing to check. Still looking the girl in the face, the uniformed man slid his hand down Maddy's tummy to the lips of her auburn shrouded sex. As he seized them, Maddy let out a small cry. She felt him rub the lips gently, tickling the button at their joining. Maddy grimaced. It was yet another insult to her flesh. She could not avoid the gaze of the man who fondled her. And she could not prevent the tingling that began in her loins or the lubrication of her wide open slit. Tears crept down her face slowly as she swayed slightly in her chins. She dared a minor imprecation, "Please," was all she said, her voice low, almost a whisper.

"Shut up, cunt," the man said.

Maddy shut her eyes and her mouth. It was useless to plead with these people. They had her fate in their hands and she was powerless.

The effects of the manipulation of her pussy soon had its intended effect on the girl. She tried to stretch her legs, standing on her tip toes, to assuage the slowly building sensations. Involuntarily, her hips began to rock. Her chest was blotched with redness, the nipples of her swaying breasts hardened. She could neither avoid the man's stimulation of her sex nor speed it. Either one would have been preferable to the slow, inexorable build up of her passions. She opened her eyes to see the man still staring at her face. Herman and Louise were watching, like trainers monitoring the performance of a dog they were selling. Maddy could not restrain herself any more. She raised and lowered her hips in a strange mimic of fucking. She was breathing deeply, tiny cries escaping from her lips.

Maddy was grateful when her explosion of lust overcame her. "Oh! Oh! Oh!" she cried. Her juices flooded the hand that tormented her. Her whole body shook with pleasure. For a moment, and only a moment, Maddy forgot where she was, what was happening to her. She uttered a long, deep, moaning sigh.

When Maddy recovered, the man was still looking into her face. But now he was smiling. "That's a good girl," he said. Maddy was mortified and humiliated. A wave of disconsolation passed through her. She was going to be this man's prisoner. "What I have ever done to deserve this?" she thought miserably.

The man brought his sticky hand to Maddy's lips. "Clean it!" he ordered.

Maddy looked over at Hermann, who had the wand. She looked at the man in front of her. What choice did she have? She licked her own discharge off of the man's hand. When she had finished to his satisfaction, the man stepped back. "She'll do fine," he said. He nodded to Herman and moved on to the next girl. Herman stepped forward, reinserted the ball in her unhappy mouth and drew the hood back over her head.

Maddy heard the man's callous comments about Peggy Ann, who was next to her. "Small tits," he said. "A little heavy in the hips. Nice ass though. Let's see her face."

The man approved of Peggy Ann's facial appearance and then put her through the same sexual exercise as Maddy. Maddy heard the girl's squeals and whines as she was driven to orgasm. Peggy Ann was a screamer and she called out loudly as she came. "Oh God! Oh God! Oh! Oh! Oh!" She, too, was ordered to lick her pungent cum off of the man's hand. The man made a sound of approval.

The man was not quite so sanguine when he came to examine the blond girl. "She's skinny," he said with disdain.

"She'll fill out," Herman answered. "She's been in the hole for two weeks," he lied.

"I don't think so," the man answered. "Let's see her face."

Louise cooperatively removed the hood and the ball. As soon as her gag was removed the girl began to beg and plead.

"Oh, please let me go, please. I want to go, please, please let me go!"

Maddy heard a resounding "crack" as the man evidently slapped her in the face. "Shut the fuck up!" he yelled. But that didn't stop the girl.

"Ahhhhhhhhh!" she cried. "Oh, god, don't hit me please! I want to go home! Please let me go!"

"Gimme that thing," the man growled to Herman. Herman handed him the wand. 'Zap!' The man shocked her loins.

"Eeeeeeeeeeee!" the young girl screeched.

'Zap!' Another scream. 'Zap!' Another scream.

The wand was placed in the girl's cunt one more time.

"Oh, no!" she screamed desperately. "I'll be good, I'll be good! Please don't hurt me anymore! Please!"

The man spoke to her sternly, "Then shut the fuck up! Got it?"

"Oh, yes, yes! I'll be quiet."

"Shut the fuck up!" the man roared.

Finally, the little blond girl was silent. Maddy could hear her sniffling and a low whine.

"Where the fuck did you get her?" the man asked.

"She was a waitress at a diner. She's over eighteen. She's pretty. I'll bet she fucks like there was no tomorrow," Herman replied.

"Yeah? Did you fuck her?" the man asked.

"No way," Herman replied. "Honest."

The man took another long look at the girl. "Well, I know a guy, maybe, okay."

"Don't you want to make her come?" Herman asked.

"She won't do too much fuckin' where I'm sending her," the man explained. "Not for too long, anyway."

"Let's go in the house and work out the details," Herman said.

"Okay," the man answered. He and Herman departed.

The young guy had watched quietly while his boss appraised the merchandise. He watched as Louise regagged and hooded the blond girl. He then turned and, leaving the barn, went to the truck. He dug behind a couple of rows of boxes of uniform pants and took a specially marked box out of the van. He manhandled it back into the barn and placed it on the floor. Opening it, he removed three wide belts. He took the first to Maddy and, circling her waist with it, locked it into position. Its hasp closed easily but was removable only with a key. He placed a similar belt on the two other naked women. He looked over at Louise.

"Can you unhook them for me?" he asked.

"Sure can," Louise said. "Which one first?"

"The screamer, I guess," the bulky youth answered.

Louise stepped over and released the lock that held the blond girl's yoke together. The girl stumbled due to the spreader bar and her blindness, but her neck and hands were freed. Louise held her up. The heavy man removed two bracelets from the box and installed them on the blond girl's wrists. He then affixed the wrists to the side of the belt. The belt was pulled taut, just above the girl's hips. It could be slid down, with some difficulty. The next accessory was meant to prevent that. A jumble of leather straps was removed from the box. He took it over to the whining girl and dropped it on the floor in front of her. He turned to Louise. "The collar?"

"Yeah, I'll get it off," she answered. She took a key from a ring she kept in her dress pocket and removed the narrow collar. She put it on a hook on the wall of the barn. She would take them all downstairs later.

While the naked, blond girl stood there helplessly, the man wrapped a leather band around her neck. It was a quarter inch thick and was attached to straps fore and aft. He ran the front strap down between the blonde's tiny breasts and fastened it to the front of the belt. He pulled it tight. He then repeated the process in the back. Now the belt was immovable.

The spreader bar was removed and bracelets were applied to her ankles connected by a 18" long chain. The man paused. It was time to do the head.

Returning to the box, the man brought back a leather helmet like device. Louise, in anticipation of his needs, removed the hood and the ball gag. The blond girl looked about wildly. She saw the thing in the man's hands and guessed its purpose. "Please don't put that thing on me?" she asked piteously. "Please?"

"Shut the fuck up," the man said. The blond girl complied. Her body was shivering with fright. What had the man meant that she wouldn't do too much fucking? What were they going to do with her? As the man presented a large leather plug to her mouth she moaned loudly. "Oh, god, no!"

The man rammed the gag home. It filled her mouth. Her cheeks actually bulged. Her lips were distended gruesomely. The gag was attached to a hood that went over the girl's face. It buckled under her chin and covered her head with leather. Two small plugs went into her ears to inhibit her reception of sound. There were two little straps that allowed their adjustment for her small head, two little holes for her to breathe through her nose. Her eyes were covered.

There was one last device to be affixed on the girl's body. The young man took another belt from the box. It was also made of leather, but had a thick absorbent pad almost its entire length. The man snaked it between the blond girl's thighs and attached it to the front and back of the belt. Accidents might happen, and they didn't want the truck all fouled up. In fact, the girls would almost certainly have to pee several times during the fifteen hour trip to New Jersey.

When it was her turn to be prepared, Maddy docilely allowed the confining outfit to be installed on her body. She knew resistance was futile, as was any effort to obtain mercy. Her fate was sealed, whatever it was. She didn't start to cry until the leather hood had been pulled over her head and attached under her chin. But her tears were remarked by no one but herself, as the salty drops were absorbed by the thick leather of the hood.

The tall, distraught girl was led from the barn to the van. As he had done with the other girls, the man patiently tugged on the girl's arm, letting her progress slowly, with tiny steps, to the transport. Girls who were trussed up like this were rarely uncooperative. What choice did they have?

Once at the van, the man pulled Maddy forward so that her torso fell across his back. He then lifted her into the van. There was another short passage and Maddy thought she heard the faint noise of what sounded like a locker door opening. Almost all sound was suppressed by the earplugs. She was shoved inside and straps tightened about her neck, chest, thighs and ankles. She heard the locker door slam shut with a deadened, 'clang'.

The lockers at the sides of the van's interior were barely distinguishable from the walls. The walls had been built out to accommodate the nine inches or so that was the average measurement, front to back, of the female body. Girls with torsos a little bit thicker got squeezed in.

The heavy set man was done. He wanted a beer but would accept the coffee that was proffered earlier.

While the younger man was loading the truck, the older man was settling accounts with Herman. The price on the tall girl had been set. It had been listed with the want notice that had been emailed to Herman a month or so ago over a secure server. But the prices on the other two were open to negotiation.

Herman faced a somewhat loaded deck. The girls were being packed for shipment already. Even if he didn't like the price, there were not a lot of people to sell them to. In fact, these people he was dealing with would take it hard if he started selling to anyone else. But ultimately, usually, a fair price was reached. After all, the buyers wanted Herman to keep collecting girls for them. So they had to pay him commensurate with the risk. There were not a lot of sources of fine, young, female flesh, and few as good at supplying it as Herman and Louise.

Herman had made coffee. As he poured the tall man a cup he asked him, "Well, what do you think the little one's worth." He wanted to settle her price first and then bargain up for the cheerleader. She actually was a cheerleader, from the University of Alabama. Herman had watched her pretty panties as she had been flung into the air by her teammates. He was sold on her at once.

The tall man knew his business. It was the cheerleader first.

"I'll give you $25,000 for the brunette."

"She's worth more than that," Herman replied. Both men knew that this was true. But bargaining was bargaining.

"Her tits are small," the tall man said as he took a first sip of his coffee.

"Not that small," Herman answered. "And she's got a great ass. You said so yourself."

"A nice ass I said."

"Better than nice."

"Okay, better than nice. But look what we paid you last time for the black haired girl. Now, she had an ass, and we only gave you $35,000 for her."

The bargaining continued for a while. They settled on $30,000 for the cheerleader. The tall man offered $15,000 for the blond. Herman cursed himself for not taming her a little while he had her in the 'hole'. That awful screaming! And the mouth! He should have taught her to keep it closed. Well, it was still all profit.

"I'll let you have her for $17,500," he said grudgingly. Both men knew that this was fair.

"Done."

The agreed upon price for the tall girl was $50,000. "Somebody wants this girl real bad," Herman thought to himself when he got the email. Well, he wanted 50 grand pretty bad. He had determined he would find the perfect girl and he had.

The tall man counted out $97,500, 975 hundred dollar bills, 19 packs of fifty, plus twenty five on the side. Herman left it there while they talked. He would recount every pack later.

"So, Herman," the man asked, "you staying in business?"

"Sure, why not?" Herman answered. No way would he ever tell this guy he was retiring. If he told them that, he would no longer be of any use to them, he was more than likely to get a bullet behind the ear first. But he wanted one more score. One more good payday, and he was out. "I'll have another load for you in two weeks," he said.

CHAPTER SIX

Martinez took a long drink of coffee. The stake out had been a waste of time. He knew it would be, but Jake was the boss and he got paid no matter what. They were back in the conference room again. It was 11 A.M. There had been progress.

Jake had reported to Burnham the night before and he would call him again after the conference. Always keep the customer informed. That way, if something went wrong, you didn't have to explain it from the beginning.

Martinez was a light skinned Latino. He had black hair and a small, narrow mustache. He was light and wiry. He was sharp as a tack and was a good watcher. He had a great sense of people and could pick out a baddun from a block away. If he didn't see anybody suspicious, then they just weren't there. He spoke Spanish, of course, but also Portuguese, Italian, some French and a smattering of Swedish. Where that last one came from no one knew. And, consistent with type, he was aces with a knife.

"So, boss," he said, "where we at?"

Jake leaned back in his chair. He looked over at his techie. "Well, Irving," he inquired, "where are we at?"

Irving took a deep breath and shuffled a small stack of papers in front of him. He had worked most of the night assembling in his mind the necessary components of the 'gizmo', as he called it, which apparently cut off the gas to Maddy's car. "I figured out two ways to assemble the gizmo you'd need to clamp off the gas by radio control," he said. "You'd need to have a strong transmitter and a sensitive receiver because of the electrical current being thrown off in the engine compartment. Transmitters that strong are a dime a dozen, but there are only two receivers made that are durable enough and small enough to work. Don't forget that you can't predict with any real assurance that the car won't go over a pothole or down a bumpy road, or even get rear ended by somebody."

"Come on, Irving, I don't need the lecture, just give me what you've got." Jake insisted.

"Okay, okay. But you've got to hear it all. You want to have confidence in my conclusions, don't you? I mean I can see it now, 'Are you sure, Irving? How do you know that, Irving? What makes you so certain, Irving?' Jeez!" Irving was easily exasperated.

"My bad, Irving," Jake said. "Get on with it."

"Okay. I ruled out one of the receivers since it's got a poor record for durability. A real good receiver, but not one that you want to knock around. The receiver I would have used is made by Raytheon and is carried by three electronic catalogues and two electronic chains."

"Give me their names and I'll get somebody working on checking it out," Jake said.

"Hold on, cowboy, there's more."

Jake looked at Irving, exasperated. "So, give," he said impatiently.

"I sent out the vacuumed stuff from the car and the clay from the tote bag. The vacuumed stuff so far is a dud. But that'll take a while yet to go all the way through. And anyway, the stupid flatfoots were all over the inside of the car so I don't expect anything too useful from that."

Irving took a sip of his coffee. Everyone else rolled their eyes. Irving had a flair for the dramatic.

"The clay, however, was a home run," he continued. "It's Georgia clay, as I expected. Now where would a girl from Carter County, Tennessee get Georgia clay on her tote bag? I think that the bag was in the guy's car for some reason. While it was there, probably on the floor, it picked up the clay. After he made the snatch, he threw it back in the car. He probably had to open the hood from the inside anyway to retrieve the gizmo."

"Well, Irving, Georgia's a pretty big state." Martinez knew his geography.

"Ah, yes, Senor Martinez, but what we have to find is overlapping sets. One set is the places in Georgia where this kind of clay is found. There are about twenty five locations mapped by the state geological survey."

"And the other set, I suppose," Jake said, "is the stores that carry this receiver."

"Yes, and it gets better," Irving replied. "You see, I run one of the best labs in the country. I hire the best guys I can find. Cost is no....."

"Enough with the commercial, Irving," Jake interrupted. "Give."

Tucker was in a distracted state. Any heavy thinking like this made his mind fog up. Just give him somebody's face to smash. The other two men were hanging on Irving's every word.

"Well, the clay deposits of this particular type run down along the banks of the Chattahoochee River. It's three hundred miles from the mountains to the sea. But we found something that narrows it down considerably. My guys found a trace of a juniper berry in the clay. Just a little tiny piece, probably from an exploded pod. Well, there's only about a ten mile stretch along the river where this variety of juniper bushes grow, just south of West Point Lake on the Alabama border."

"You mean that this guy lives somewhere in that ten mile stretch?" Martinez asked.

"Not necessarily," Irving answered. "He could have gotten out of his car to take a piss there. But it's at least even money. And, it gets better."

"Irving, you're killing me," Jake complained.

"I know," Irving replied, "But I can't help it. So anyway, remember when I said that there were two chains that carried the receiver?"

"We remember!" Jake and Martinez said at the same time.

"Well, there's only one store within fifty miles of this clay and the juniper trees. That's in Colombus."

"Okay," Jake said with authority. "Martinez, get on the phone and check out the store see if they sold one of these things."

"Not so fast, Count," Irving interjected. "I have the solution right here." He pointed to his stack of papers. "One of these receivers was sold by the Columbus store three months ago."

"Three months ago!" Jake exclaimed. "What good is that?"

"Listen, they only sell a few hundred of these things a year in the entire country, outside of the military, that is."

"The military?" Jake asked. "Isn't there a military base near Colombus?"

"Yeah," Martinez answered. "It's called Fort Benning."

"Fort Benning? Congratulations Irving, you've narrowed it down to somebody in the 3rd Infantry Division!" Jake was not happy being led down a garden path.

"No, no, no," Irving replied. "This guy isn't in the military."

"Come on, Irving, now you're working on a hunch," Jake said.

"Yes, a hunch," Irving replied, "but a good one. You've got to have a lot of free time to go around snatching girls."

"One girl," Jake retorted.

"I'm betting there are more," Irving answered.

"I'm still waiting for a response from my FBI contact. So the jury's still out on that," Jake said.

"Listen, the profile for this type of guy doesn't fit the military," Irving continued. "He's a white guy, between 45 and 60. He probably lives somewhere remote and alone. If he's killing these girls, he's got to have a lot of property to bury them, otherwise there'd be bodies turning up everywhere."

"Okay, that's enough on that for now," Jake announced. "I'm going to wait until I hear from the FBI guy before I jump on that with both feet. In the meantime," Jake said turning to Martinez, "I assume the college angle is a dead end."

"Yeah, it's a dead end. It just doesn't feel right."

"Oh?" Irving interrupted. "Now who's got the hunch?"

"It's a hunch I can live with. I'm pretty well convinced on the Georgia angle," Jake stated. "The store in Columbus is a good lead. In the meantime, I'm going to talk to the mechanic. I want to tie down this 'gizmo' thing. If this guy says he put a clamp on that hose for any reason, we're back to square one."

The other men in the room nodded. Even Tucker understood this one.

"I want all the stores and catalogue places checked anyway. Irving, can you tap into the catalogue company computers?"

"Easily," he answered.

"Then do it. Martinez and Tucker, I want you guys to go down to Columbus and nose around. Get me the feel of the place and scout out this ten mile corridor." Jake turned to Irving. "How wide is it?"

"Oh, maybe five miles," he answered.

"Great, we've got fifty square miles to cover. Anyway, we can start, but I don't want to put all of our eggs in one basket. Tomorrow I'm going down to Fort Benning to look around. Let me tell you that an infantry division has about 10,000 guys. And there's all kinds of support people. Let's hope Irving is right about the clay and his profile of the kidnapper. And let's hope that our guy just didn't stop to take a piss on the side of the road."

* * * * * * * * * * *

The delivery van rolled inexorably towards Elizabeth, New Jersey with its three dismayed passengers. Maddy had no idea how long she had been cooped up in the locker, but she had already peed twice. She raged against the people who were so mistreating her, schemed of possible escapes. She thought of her father, of Harold, her ex-boyfriend, of her friends. She thought back to Jefferson High in Cleveland. She tried to think about anything but where she was headed and what would happen to her when she got there. When she did, and she could not help but think of it, she had a cold, sinking feeling in her stomach.

She was grateful when the gentle rocking of the truck along the highway lulled her to sleep. She drifted in and out for long periods, or what seemed to be long periods, since she had no way of keeping time. She had no idea whether they had been on the road for three, four or ten hours. It seemed like forever.

The men in the front of the truck were taking turns driving. The tall one drove first. After three hours, Chuckie, the younger guy, took over.

"Hey Mr. Feeney, when are we gonna eat?" he asked.

'Feeney' was all anyone knew him by. It was 'Mr. Feeney' to the guys who worked for him. He shook himself awake. "Eat?" he replied. "Is that all you can think about, food?"

"No, I give an awful lot of thought to the cunts in the back of the truck too. How I wanna fuck em."

"Well stop thinking about it, got it?" Feeney said, annoyed. "You'll get some poontang when we get to Elizabeth."

"We shouda bought that cunt he had in the hole," Chuckie continued.

"Are you kidding?" Feeney asked. "I already got one bitch I'm gonna have a hard time gettin' rid of."

"Yeah, but we coulda kept the fat girl around for a while, you know, fuck meat."

Chuckie and Feeney had been invited down in the 'hole' for a blow job before they left. Maureen was quite shocked to see new people. When she was told to suck their cocks, she thought that maybe if she did a good job she would get taken away by them. She wasn't that fat and she had lost at least ten pounds since she had been kidnapped.

Herman pulled Maureen's head through the little window in the cage and then fastened the back of her collar to the topmost bar. Feeney had gone first. It was against his better judgment, but all that pussy juice he had smelled had really gotten him horny. The girl slurped and slobbered over his dick. She hadn't been taught how to give a good blowjob yet. They say that there is no such thing as a bad blowjob, but this was as close as it got. He had to grab her head and pump his cock down her throat to get off.

Chuckie had a very different experience. He loved the slippery warmth of Maureen's mouth. He liked how she worked so hard to pleasure him. She made a little humming sound as she sucked him, staccato-like. Each time she bobbed her head down on his cock she uttered a little "mmmmmm." It didn't take long for him to flood her mouth with jism. It dribbled down her chin. Chuckie laughed. He took some in his hand and smeared it over her face.

The desperate fat girl was disconsolate when Herman shoved the gag back in. He unhooked her collar from the steel framework and pushed her head back so that she fell against the back of the cage. Frantic, Maureen threw herself against the cage's front. Her words were garbled, but their import was clear.

Herman smelt an income opportunity. "I could let you have her for another ten grand," he said hopefully.

"No thanks," Feeney replied as he climbed up the ladder.

"$5,000?" Herman inquired. He didn't want to give up his fuck bunny for so little but, money was money and five grand was five grand.

"No," was all that Feeney said.

Chuckie just shrugged his shoulders and zipped up. "Goodbye, suckbucket," he said to Maureen and launched himself up the stairs.

Herman leaned over the cage and said ominously, "I'll be back, suckbucket."

So Feeney and Chuckie had divergent views on the value of Maureen, but it was Feeney's opinion that counted. And now that Chuckie had mentioned it, he was a little hungry too. It would be good to stretch their legs.

"Okay, next time you see a McDonalds or Burger King, or some place like that, you can pull over."

They were traveling North on Route 81 in Virginia. They had been on the road for about six hours. Ironically, they passed within a mile of Maddy's apartment as they passed through Carter County, Tennessee. She had no way of knowing that and never would.

Maddy felt the truck come to a rolling stop. It jolted her awake. Maybe they had reached their destination. Maybe the truck had been stopped by the cops. Should she do something? Anything? The only part of her that she could move was her head. Her arms and legs were fastened down prohibitively. She tried to bang her head against the back of the locker, but the place behind her head was heavily padded. She could feel her head hitting the pad, but she couldn't tell if she was making any noise. The earplugs shut it all out.

Feeney got out and lit a cigarette. He hated smoking while he rode in a car; it made him queasy. Chuckie hopped out and headed for the restaurant.

"Hey, where you goin'?" Feeney called to him.

"I got to piss, bad," Chuckie answered.

"Okay, but just get some food and come right back out. Get me a double cheeseburger and a Coke."

Chuckie just waved in response and kept walking.

Feeney took a tour around the van to make sure that everything was copasetic. He stopped for a moment, thinking that he heard something from inside. He knew the girls were tied in tight. The little cells were well insulated. The truck pumped air in and out. He listened carefully a moment more. "Nah," he thought to himself. He was mistaken.

Maddy stopped banging her head and started to sob. What was happening to her was unbelievable. Every girl holds a secret, or not so secret, fear of being raped or murdered. Or being raped and murdered. But to be kidnapped like this, to be bought and sold? How could she ever have prepared herself for this? It was only the resumption of the vibration of the truck's engine and its return to motion that ceased Maddy's crying. Apparently they were not yet at their destination. She had a reprieve from her fate.

It was 1 o'clock in the afternoon when the van finally arrived in Elizabeth. Feeney was driving and he had about had it. "Maybe next time I'll bring two guys," he thought. "This driving is killing me."

The van pulled into the garage of the Nationwide Uniform Company. There were uniform trucks pulling in and out. If anybody had checked on the van while on the road, it would have come back perfectly legit. There was a special interior door in the garage that was used only by special vans. Feeney had the remote for the door and pressed it. The door lurched open. He drove the van through to another door. He waited until the rear door was closed and then got down and punched a combination into the controller for that door. It started to rise and he jumped back into the truck and drove it through. The door closed automatically.

The second door led to a long ramp downwards. Once the van reached the bottom, Feeney shut the engine and stepped out. "Home at last," he thought.

Chuckie stepped out of the other side. "Hey, Mr. Feeney, I'm really bushed. Can we leave the goods in the truck until later?" he asked, yawning.

"Absolutely not, idiot. They'd suffocate in about an hour," Feeney answered in an aggravated tone. "Come on, it'll take fifteen minutes."

Feeney unlocked the back of the van and hopped up inside. Each cell, or locker, as you might want to call it, had its own lock. From the outside, you couldn't even tell it was there. You had to slide a little lever here and pull another one there and the lock was exposed. The door looked just like a seam in the wall.

Maddy felt the cool air as the door to her locker was opened. She began to shake, terrified of what was to happen next. She felt the straps being undone about her and then her body pulled out of the locker. The chain was still affixed to her ankles and she stumbled as she tried to take a step. Feeney pulled her along gently until she was at the edge of the truck. He then pushed her forward and she fell onto Chuckie's shoulder. Chuckie let her down and then walked her over to a steel door. He left her standing there.

The girl was totally disorientated. Not to be fastened to anything, or inside anything, was a strange sensation. Her wrists were affixed to her sides. She clenched her useless hands in frustration. Maddy felt someone bump up against her. It was naked flesh, an arm, or a shoulder. A few more minutes passed and then she was moving ahead again. She stepped over a little bump and stopped. She then proceeded once more and then was carried down a short flight of stairs.

Maddy had entered the holding area of what was essentially a slave transfer station. She had passed through a large, windowless, steel door. The room she was let into was long and narrow. Low cages lined one side, twenty in all. There was a long, thick pipe that ran the length of the room along the twelve foot high ceiling, with big knobs at either end. A ring passed around the pipe, which was attached to a chain. The chain descended to where it was attached to the steel collar of a naked, raven haired young woman. She was kneeling on the floor, her head bowed.

Feeney addressed her. "I want you to put these three cunts in cages. Water them, change their pads, and put the gags and hoods back in when you're finished. Got that?"

"Yes master," the supine young girl intoned without looking up.

Feeney spoke to Chuckie, "Come on, let's get a drink." The two men left, carefully double locking each steel door.

The three girls could hear murmurings going on outside them, but nothing else. Maddy felt herself being pulled along by what felt like a feminine hand. She walked about fifteen feet and then was pushed to her knees. There was a short cessation of motion during which she felt a naked body lean up against her. She was then pushed backwards. She fell over and into something. The hands pushed at her legs, stuffing them in. Maddy tried to rise to her knees. Her head hit something. She moved forward and felt thin, cold steel bars. She was caged!

The black haired slave girl took her time, but remorselessly caged each of the women in turn. When she was done, she walked slowly to the other end of the room, her chain tailing behind her, sliding along the pipe attached to the ceiling. At the rear of the room, she retrieved a cart holding a plastic bottle of water, a bucket, soap and some sponges, a dry cotton towel, a container of lotion, and some pads. She filled the bucket with cold water from a steel spigot and trudged back to where the three girls were imprisoned.

This was Allison. She was the caretaker of this little dungeon. Out of the twenty cages, seven of them were filled with bound, naked, gagged and hooded young women. Now there were ten. Allison's job was to care for these incipient slaves in transit. She had been here a long time, longer than she could remember. This dungeon was her complete world. The only human contact, other than that of her slavish charges, was when one of the masters came down to fuck her or to beat her. She preferred being fucked.

Maddy sensed her cage door opening and felt herself pulled forwards. Hands fiddled with the hood over her head and then it was removed. She was shocked to see the naked and chained young woman. She noted with apprehension the long chain that connected the woman to the pipe on the ceiling. The girl loosened Maddy's gag and removed it from her mouth. Maddy was overwhelmed with relief to be freed of the brutal instrument that had silenced her. She sucked greedily at the bottle of tepid water that the girl presented to her mouth. The water tasted like heaven as it soothed her parched throat. When the girl withdrew the bottle, Maddy tried to speak to her.

"Where am I?" she asked, her fear evident in her voice. The black haired girl did not reply, but unleashed a violent slap across Maddy's face.

"Shut up!" she ordered forcefully.

Maddy's head was turned by the blow and she felt the sting of the girl's hand on her face. "Oh!" she cried. The girl pulled on Maddy's collar and brought her back to facing her. Without speaking, she proffered the gag back to Maddy's mouth. Tearfully, in acknowledgement of her powerless state, Maddy accepted it.

The girl pushed Maddy backwards into the cage and motioned for her to turn around. Maddy knew what was wanted. She had turned her back this way many times to Louise. Maddy placed her head down and spread her thighs. She felt the cotton pad being removed from between her legs. Allison used the sponge to apply cold, soapy water to her loins. She was dried with the towel and soothing lotion applied. Another pad was installed. The girl pulled her around again and reapplied the noxious hood.

About an hour after the black haired girl had finished her attentions to the new girls, Feeney returned. Chuckie had gone off to find some "poontang" as he called it. There was plenty for sale in this part of town. Feeney was in the market for a blow job and bed. He walked slowly down the corridor of naked and confined women. He wasn't interested in the slave girl tonight. He could have her anytime. All of the girls were appealing. Their hoods and ear plugs made them oblivious to his observation of them. Most of them lay listlessly in their cages, waiting for their next feeding or a cold shower from a hose wielded by the black haired girl. A few nodded and swayed their heads and torsos rhythmically. They were starved for sensation, and even the feeling of their bodies in motion was better than nothing. It was similar to the behavior of caged animals, creatures incapable of understanding the nature and purpose of their captivity.

Feeney stopped by Maddy's cage. The tall young woman was cruelly confined in the small cage. She was lying on her side, her knees up to her chest. Feeney recalled her thick, red lips from the night before. She had tempting, large breasts. She would do.

He called for the slave girl to drag Maddy from her cage. When Maddy felt the prodding of the girl's hands, she recoiled. When the girl began to pull on her arm, Maddy, realizing the fruitlessness of resistance, allowed herself to be guided to the cage door and out.

Maddy felt cold, coarse concrete on her knees. The hood was removed and she saw the cruel face of her tormentor of the night before. He was smiling at her. The black haired girl knelt next to Maddy, awaiting instructions.

"Get her gag off," Feeney told the slave girl. She unbuckled it from behind Maddy's head and pulled the leather plug free. Feeney began to loosen his fly.

"Time for a blow job, slut," he said to Maddy. "You know how to give a blow job, don't you?"

Grimacing, Maddy nodded 'yes'. She knew better than to talk. She looked nervously around her. It was the first time she had gotten a good look at the dungeon. The sight of nine other naked and caged women unnerved her. The dark grey, windowless, cinderblock walls oppressed her. "What is all this for?" she asked herself. "What is going to happen to me?"

Feeney had his skinny, but long, cock out now and was manipulating it to hardness. He looked at Maddy coldly. "Get your lips on my meat, cunt," he ordered.

Maddy edged herself closer to the tall, thin man. Tears rolled down her cheeks. She opened her mouth and tentatively circled her lips around the man's now hard joint. There was no sense in fighting him. Maddy abhorred pain and was sure a painful beating would be the price of resistance. The sooner she started, the sooner she would be done.

Feeney addressed the slave girl. "remove her pad and rub her cunt while she sucks me off," he told her. Maddy, the man's long cock now fully in her mouth, felt the black haired girl's body press up against hers. She felt her hand snake between her thighs, slip off the pad that covered her mons and seize her nether lips. A long, boney finger pierced them and drew itself along the length of her slit, coming to rest on the little nubbin of pleasure at the apex to her sex. As she felt the girl gently tickle her clit, Maddy moaned with unexpected pleasure.

Maddy tried to concentrate on her unpleasant task. She bobbed her head back and forth, teasing the shaft of Feeney's cock with her tongue. Her sophomore boyfriend, Buddy, had taught her how to suck a cock, and she had built on the knowledge she had gained from him over the years. She liked to use her hands to coax the hot sperm from the little sac and to hold the shaft steady while she swirled her lips and her tongue over the bulbous head. Even without the use of her hands, though, she soon had Feeney moaning with pleasure.

The black haired girl's efforts were having their effect on Maddy, too. She could feel the girl's breasts rubbing up against her arm as she pleasured her now moist and soft pussy with her hand. Maddy tried to suppress the heat that crept up from her loins. She didn't want to come for this cruel bastard. She wanted to preserve some dignity. But it was not to be.

Maddy felt a surge of heat roll over her. Her eyes were clamped shut in an attempt to block out her dismal surroundings and the image of the man whose cock was invading her mouth. Feeney placed his hands on her head and began to thrust into her. He rammed his cock against the back of her mouth ruthlessly. Bit by bit, Maddy's blood rose. Finally, all else was forgotten except the pleasure she was receiving from the hand on and in her hot gash and the hard meat in her mouth. Maddy started to cry out, short, high pitched cries. When her pussy began to throb and contract, her orgasm upon her, she moaned and thrust her hips forwards. Her body shuddered, her breasts swayed and jerked. It was too much for Feeney and his cock began to spurt its hot load into Maddy's mouth. "Oh! Oh! Oh!" he cried, as the shocks of his climax reverberated through his body.

Feeney patted Maddy's cheek lightly. "Good girl," he said. He nodded to Allison and she pulled Maddy back over to her cage. Maddy's eyes were filled with tears as the gag was reinserted and the hood descended over her head. Her little diaper-like pad was reinstalled. She allowed herself to be pushed back into the cage.

Maddy went through several cycles of being washed and fed. Once a day, she was taken to the rear of the room and given an enema. Her hands remained constantly confined to the leather belt that encircled her waist. Allison fed the women twice a day. This necessitated the removal of the hood and gag. On the second day, Maddy noted that the cage next to hers, the one that had contained the skinny blond, the screamer, was empty. The next day it was full again.

The days were long and enervating. Maddy could hear the muffled sound of what appeared to be random activity in the cellar dungeon, but had little clue as to what actually was going on. For what seemed hours at a time, there was no sound at all, as the plugs in her ears blocked the stifled murmurings that emerged from the prisoners' gags. Once, she thought she heard the screaming of a woman in pain, begging and pleading for mercy.

The only real activity was when she was washed and fed by the black haired 'trustee'. Maddy did not make the mistake of speaking to her again, but she could not help cry each time the girl proffered back the heinous gag and reinstalled the evil hood that blocked out all sight and almost all sound. Back in her cell after a washing and feeding, Maddy would scrunch her body into the smallest ball she could make and sob.

Maddy thought often of how she might be saved. She thought of her rich uncle in New York. Maybe somehow he could discover what had happened to her and purchase her freedom. Maybe the police, the FBI, someone, would track down her kidnappers and save her. Maybe she could find some way to escape.

During her confinement, Maddy went over in her mind time and time again the last moments of her freedom. She could still see the face of the old woman smiling at her. She cursed herself for a fool for having gotten out of the car, for not calling the police. She cursed herself for her weakness in failing to fight off her kidnappers. She cursed herself for abjectly sucking that man's prick, the one who had bought her, and not biting it off.

The days were long and incredibly lonely. The only face she saw was the stone hard features of the black haired girl. She yearned to talk to someone, share her sorrow, her hopelessness. She couldn't even use her hands to scratch herself when she itched. She didn't know whether it was night or day. She could only count her feedings, and she could not even tell how many times a day she was fed or whether she was fed at regular intervals.

On what Maddy took to be the fourth day, she was dragged from her cage. She felt the presence of men around her and she could hear their low toned voices, muffled by the plugs in her ears. She had not been used since her first day in this hellhole, but she knew that she was helpless and that somehow her kidnapping and her cruel imprisonment was a prelude to her eventual rape and ravishment. Why else would she be caged and isolated amidst other naked and bound women? The men who had bought her from her kidnappers were slavers, she realized that now. Where and whom she would serve was unknown to her, but the reality of her dismal future had sunk in over hours of silent, enforced contemplation.

When Maddy realized that she was being taken somewhere by strange men, she felt her stomach turn. Was this to be the moment of truth where all would be revealed? Or was she merely being led to some torture chamber where she would be abused unmercifully?

She felt a strong, masculine hand on her arm. Her ankles were rehobbled and she was led from the room, shuffling along like a convict on a chain gang.

The frightened girl was led back into the receiving area where she had been unloaded from the van. There her hood was removed. She saw before her what appeared to be a long, silver coffin. Its lid was off and there was no question but that it was meant for her.

Maddy, for the first time in her captivity, began to struggle in earnest. She did not know that five of the caged girls had gone before her and that their aluminum containers were already stacked on the truck. All she knew was that they were going to lock her in a coffin.

The men who were handling Maddy were well prepared for her resistance. All of the girls reacted the same way when they saw the forbidding, coffin-like object. The men held on to Maddy's arms and pulled her towards her apparent doom. In fact, the 'coffin' was a shipping container. It had a series of straps and belts meant to keep quiescent its occupant. A specially designed mask would serve the salutary purposes of silencing the packaged woman and maintaining a flow of oxygen.

Maddy was unceremoniously dragged to a small padded stool and pushed to her knees in front of it. The poor girl was wailing and sobbing like there was no tomorrow. From Maddy's point of view, from what she could discern, there would be no tomorrow. Her strange journey and stranger confinement was about to end in a burial alive!

The men pushed Maddy down over the padded stool and held her still. Due to her frantic state, it took three of them. She felt a jab in her right buttock and the sensation of a drug being injected into her body. It took only a few seconds and the girl's head began to fog. She was held down over the stool for several minutes. By the time the men released her, her limbs had gone limp and her eyes had rolled back into her head. Her excited and futile wailings had been reduced to a rhythmic, sonorous moan.

When they were satisfied that they would meet with no further resistance, Maddy was carried over to her awaiting shipping case. They released her ankles from the hobble, removed her collar, belt and the leather harness and bracelets that she had been wearing, and lay her down inside the shiny crate's padded interior. Her gag was removed and a mask with a wide, solid mouthpiece that filled her oral cavity, was affixed to her face. It was not unlike the mouthpieces used by scuba divers. Maddy's head was secured as was the rest of her body. The tube from the mask led outside the crate and was connected to a small oxygen tank.

After the men made sure that the mask was operating properly, one of the men brushed alcohol on the underside of Maddy's left arm and slid a catheter into a vein. The catheter was then attached to a tube running from a bottle affixed to the lid of the container. An adjustment was made and a slow, steady drip of Demerol began to flow into Maddy's body. After checking her bindings and confirming the proper operation of the intravenous flow, the men fastened the lid, locking it firmly in place. When the top was secured, it formed a hermetic seal. Nothing could get in or out except through the narrow flexible tube connected to the mask.

The coffin-like container was then lifted onto the bed of the truck where it joined its mates. The air line was reattached to a larger tank that served all of the containers.

After three more containers were loaded and stored on the truck, the signal was given to prepare to leave. A tarp was tied over the nine gleaming canisters and several dozen large boxes of work uniforms were loaded, covering and concealing the feminine cargo. The door to the outside rose and the truck pulled up the long, winding ramp to the street level.

The truck's destination was a small loading dock not far from the airport. When the truck backed up to the dock, two men emerged and, after unloading the boxes of clothing, placed the containers, one by one, on a dolly and wheeled them to a large air cargo container sitting on a flatbed truck. The interior of the container was built out to the length of the aluminum crates containing the drugged women. There were ten slots in it. The men took the coffin-like crates and slid them into the slots, feet first. They were a perfect fit. The crates were locked in and the air hoses were connected to nozzles that led to a large air tank which constituted the base of the storage unit. A heavy steel cover was affixed to the end of the unit and bolted on, effectively sealing the women in. The steel door was slammed shut and a forged inspector's seal applied. Two hours later, a heavy duty forklift loaded the air cargo container into the gaping rear of a large cargo plane. A half hour later, the plane was in the air.

CHAPTER SEVEN

Jake had questioned Danny, the mechanic, before he left for Fort Benning. Danny had confirmed that he did not work on any of Maddy's hoses when he tuned the car up a couple of weeks ago. He was affronted that Jake would even consider him responsible for the car stalling or otherwise breaking down. "That car was in tip top shape when it left here," he said, angrily, upset at the challenge to his skills. "I like that Maddy, she's real people. It'd be a real shame if anything bad happened to her."

Nodding his agreement, Jake asked Danny if had spotted anyone hanging around the bar where Maddy worked over the last couple of weeks.

"Ah, nobody goes in that place who hasn't lived here twenty years," Danny replied. He had just finished working on an engine and he was wiping grease off of his hands with a stained, red rag.

"So you haven't ever seen anyone you didn't know in there?" Jake asked incredulously.

"Oh, once in a while some good old boy will stop in for a quick one as a break from the road, but they never stay for more than a couple of beers."

"So no good old boys stopped in anytime over the last few weeks?"

"I can't say as remember any," Danny replied. "I wish I could help you. You know I...."

"You like Maddy and she's real people," Jake interrupted. "I know. Well if you think of anything, please let me know. Here's my card. Call day or night."

Jake flew a puddle jumper to a small airfield outside of Fort Benning. He had an appointment with the quartermaster of the base. He got there around four in the afternoon. He could sense that the quartermaster, a fat, slovenly, sandy haired colonel, was anxious to begin his weekend. Jake was lucky to get an interview. Michael Burnham had pulled a few strings and the colonel had agreed to see him.

"You mean a KTF stroke 7016," he said, when Jake mentioned the Raytheon miniature receiver.

"Yeah," he replied to the distracted colonel, "the KTF stroke 7016. You've got an inventory of them?"

"Sure, I checked. We've got fifteen. We had sixteen but one broke. We don't use em much. No call for them in an infantry outfit. Maybe the engineers…."

"The one that was broken, can you tell me when that was?" Jake asked, his interest piqued.

"Well, according to the SP47, Report of Casualty Loss, the piece broke on 21 January, last. two months ago. A tow motor ran over the box."

"Who signed that form, Colonel?"

"Let's see," the colonel answered. "Yeah, Master Sergeant Drake. Jarvis Drake."

"He's still here?" Jake asked.

"Oh, yeah," the colonel answered grinning. "He'll be here for a long time."

"Why's that?"

"He got killed in a jump two weeks ago. They buried him in the base cemetery. He was technically attached to the airborne school. He was qualifying for his jump pay."

"Great," Jake mumbled to himself. "What about the tow motor driver? Does the form say who he was?"

"Yes, in fact it does. A Corporal Newsome, John Newsome. He's still breathing, as far as I know."

"How can I contact him?" Jake asked.

The colonel looked at his watch. "He's just about getting off duty now. If you hurry, you'll probably catch him. He stays late a lot."

Just the kind of guy who might be taking government property out the back door, Jake thought. If Newsome sold the 'KTF stroke 7016', he might remember who bought it. Jake knew how to put pressure on a guy. Not many Quartermaster Corps. guys wanted the Inspector General's people looking through their warehouses.

Jake thanked the colonel and caught a jeep to the technology warehouse. Several soldiers were streaming out as he arrived. He asked for Corporal Newsome and was directed inside. The corporal was sitting behind a huge desk piled with paperwork. He looked up as Jake approached.

"You must be Mr. Barnes," he said. When he saw Jake's surprised look, he added, "The Colonel called me. Told me to wait for you. You have a question about a KTF stroke 7016, right?"

Jake nodded his head. His investigation wasn't going to get very far if everybody else was one step ahead of him.

"Corporal, this receiver unit that was damaged some months back, the Colonel tells me that you were driving the forklift that ran over it. Is this true?"

"Listen, Mr. Barnes, lots of stuff gets damaged in a military warehouse. And I don't particularly remember this one, small part."

Jake decided it was time to take a different tack. "Corporal, my recollection of the military tells me that corporals don't usually drive tow motors and that expensive electronic components are not usually stored on the floor. I'm involved in a very serious investigation, one that may mean the life or death of a young woman. The uncle of this woman is a very powerful man. A corporal hoping to replace a dead master sergeant as chief quartermaster for this warehouse may just want to play ball with me. The fact is that whoever stole that receiver is probably the guy who kidnapped my friend's niece."

The corporal looked up at Jake with concern. "I can guarantee you, Mr. Barnes, that that receiver unit was not involved in any kidnapping."

"Listen, Corporal," Jake said, his voice rising, "I'm from Missouri, I've got to find things out the hard way. I need proof, not a 'guarantee' from someone who's probably trying to figure out right now how much loot he can scoot out the back door of this place before the next inventory. Your master sergeant's untimely death is a golden opportunity for you. Anything missing will be pegged to him. I could make a lot of trouble for a guy pulling a scam like that."

The corporal paused, reflecting. He looked up at Jake. "Okay, okay. But you'll have to come with me."

Corporal Newsome commandeered a jeep and drove Jake across the base. They exited the main gate and drove about 45 minutes along a two lane county road. Jake fingered the Beretta in his pocket. If Newsome was in on the snatch of Madeline, he might try to ice him to buy time for a getaway. Jake would put a bullet in the corporal's brain pan first.

After about 30 minutes, the jeep pulled into a condominium complex. It skirted the buildings and was brought to a halt in the back, adjacent to a single car garage. The two men had not spoken the entire trip. Jake was in no mood for chitchat and neither, it appeared, was the corporal. Jake was sure he hit a nerve when he talked about the probable prospective and ongoing looting of the warehouse.

Newsome opened the garage door and stepped into the garage. In a few moments, he emerged with a large box. He placed the box on the ground and opened it. Inside was a two foot long scale model of a P51 Mustang, the 'Cadillac of the Skies'. Newsome removed the fighter plane from the box and brought it over to a small field that backed up to the condo development. He placed the plane on the ground, pulled a remote from the box and, in a moment, the Mustang came to life. Ten seconds later it was taxiing down the field and took off into the air.

Newsome smiled at Jake. "Custom job. It's got the best small receiver made, a KTF stroke 7016, otherwise known as a Raytheon model 2240 miniature receiver." He proffered the remote to Jake. "Want to give it a try?"

Jake smiled and shook his head. For about twenty minutes he watched the corporal take the Mustang through its paces. The show ended in a perfect, three point landing. The Fort Benning angle was a dead end.

* * * * * * * * * * *

Kalikastan is a small country the size of Montana, consisting of approximately 150,000 square miles. It is located just north of the confluence of the Don and Pfiester Rivers. While the southern part of the country, bordering on the Republic of the Ukraine, consists of vast wide open steppes, the northern half consists of gently rolling hills running eastwards and leading up to the foothills of the Urals. Its capital city boasts a population of 100,000 people. Its principal exports are oil, coal and wheat.

The country's strategic location between the southern border of the Ukraine and the long, southwestern arm of the Russian Republic, has guaranteed it a pivotal role in the economies of those two countries. Black market goods pour over its borders into its large, powerful neighbors. Its capital, Dlitski, serves as a haven for the criminal classes of both countries. It is considered neutral ground, a rule harshly enforced by the efficient Kalikastani secret police.

Since the fall of the former Soviet Union, there has developed a rather extensive and wealthy oligarchy which controls the reins of government in Kalikastan. Large estates in the hinterland serve as the conspicuous icons of wealth. And since the country was once known as the home of fierce tribes of nomadic horsemen, intolerant of government in all its forms, the midlands are more or less a law unto itself, disputes often being settled by violent gunplay between rival 'clans'.

Maddy's plane landed at Brevski Airport, about five miles outside the capital. It taxied down the long runway directly over to the air cargo customs building. The tail of the plane was cracked open and oversized forklifts began the task of removing the igloo shaped cargo containers. The first two were delivered to the customs shed to be inspected by the appropriate local officials. The third container, one that had been specially marked, was driven directly to an awaiting flatbed truck. It was covered by a large tarpaulin and driven away.

Maddy had drifted in and out of consciousness during her fifteen hour plane ride. She experienced strange physical sensations caused, unbeknownst to her, by the drift and yaw of the huge cargo plane. The jet engines caused a constant vibration that could be felt even inside the casket. But Maddy's mind never cleared sufficiently for her to draw the conclusion that she was in the air and being flown to an unknown destination thousands of miles from home.

When she finally awoke from her drug induced stupor, she was still lying in the container, its lid open, her mask and bindings still in place. The catheter had been removed, leaving a small red mark on her arm. If she could have raised and turned her head, she would have seen eight other silver caskets lined up beside her, with eight other naked and bound women attaining consciousness. Above her, she could see a high ceiling supported by crisscrossed wooden beams. She could see a faded whitewashed brick wall opposite her container. The room was deathly silent. Maddy was too weak from her ordeal to struggle, so she lay still and nervously awaited developments.

After about an hour, Maddy heard a door opening and closing and the sound of heavy boots on cement. Two unshaven, blue jeaned men, young men, no more than 25 or 26, walked past her container. She heard the men speaking in a strange language. One of the men laughed.

A cabinet was opened and Maddy heard the jingling of metal chains. After a short silence, she heard the whimper of a female voice, a word of protest and a loud slap. A harsh, male voice yelled, "Shut up, slut!" The feminine voice was stilled.

It took a little while before the men worked their way down to Maddy's container. She saw, out of the corner of her eye, the container next to her emptied, the frightened, blond haired young woman who had inhabited it drawn to her feet. The girl was crying and Maddy could hear her sniffles and sobs. One of the men, a lean, black haired man, dressed in a green t-shirt, bound the woman's hands behind her back with a leather thong, while the other clamped a four inch high steel collar around her neck. He wore a white t-shirt with a large tear along the side. He was shorter and heavier than the other man, but had similar, unruly, black hair on his head. The heavy set man clipped a three foot long chain to a ring in the front of the collar, and another to a ring on the back. The thin man had a large roll of duct tape in his hand and he tore off a long piece and fastened it over the girl's mouth.

Maddy's turn was next. When her mask was removed, she held back her urge to ask questions, the most natural one being, "Where am I?" She stared silently at the men as they undid the straps that bound her. Maddy did not want to cry, but, nonetheless, her eyes welled up and a solitary tear rolled down her face. The tall, thin man caught the droplet with his finger and, smiling, brought it to his mouth. He said something to the other man in a guttural, foreign tongue, and they both laughed.

When Maddy was brought to her feet, she saw the other women who had been bound and chained together standing, waiting expectantly for the next development. To a one, their eyes were wide with fear. None of them dared move. The men affixed the chains, collar and binding on Maddy, taped her mouth closed, and moved on to the next coffin.

It was about twenty minutes later that all the girls were chained together and ready to move. Maddy's head was still somewhat befogged by the residual of the Demerol in her system and she was unsteady on her feet. She saw the heavyset man tug the lead girl into motion. Each girl on the coffle, in turn, felt the chain pull on her neck and followed suit. The thin man walked down the line encouraging cooperation by slapping the buttocks of the naked women. The women docilely allowed themselves to be led from the long room through a door that opened to the outside.

The sun was shining brightly, having reached its noonday apex. There was a large, cobblestone courtyard outside of the building. It was surrounded on 3 sides by two storied, whitewashed, rough stone buildings with grey, slate roofs. The fourth side of the courtyard consisted of a large, stone wall with a gate in the middle of it, large enough to admit small trucks. The courtyard was buzzing with activity. There were several shiny, black Mercedes parked there, and men were walking to and fro engaged in their business. A small motorbike revved its engine and sped away through the gateway out into the unknown, to Maddy at least, world beyond.

The women were led to the center of the courtyard, the chains linking their collars released, and made to stand shoulder to shoulder. A small boy came over with a jug of water. The green shirted man took it from him and went down the line, ripping off the tape that covered the women's mouths, giving them to drink, and then replacing it. Maddy's mouth was dry and had a sour, medicinal taste. The water was cool and fresh, and she was grateful for this minor act of mercy.

The women were left standing in the hot afternoon sun for a considerable period of time. While no one stood guard over them, all of the women were too afraid to move. There was nowhere to run to anyway. It was strange to Maddy that the men who walked through the courtyard paid so little attention to them. One or two walked down the line of women, pinching a breast here and there. But, for the most part, the women were ignored, as if the presence of naked and bound women standing forlornly in the courtyard was an everyday occurrence.

Just when Maddy had begun to fear that she would collapse from exhaustion, a corpulent man, dressed in a long sleeved, striped sports shirt and sharply pressed, black trousers came walking down the wooden steps from a veranda on the second floor of the building on the women's right. He walked slowly, measuring each step carefully. He face was swarthy and he wore a thick, black, handlebar moustache. Two bulky, well dressed men accompanied him, one in front and one behind. They wore dark sports jackets and chinos. In spite of their dark sunglasses, they seemed to be consciously aware of everything around them.

All of the women's eyes were on the trio of men descending the stairs. The almost frenetic activity in the courtyard came to a halt.

Khalid Rashini had achieved prominence as the finest importer of female flesh in Kalikastan. In an almost lawless environment, he had managed to fight off every attempt to incorporate his operation into one of the vicious criminal gangs that operated freely in the country. Part of the secret of his success was his extensive family connections. But the other was the fact that the ruling cliques, who controlled the police, the army and several rather large militias, wanted a reliable and discriminating source of women to enslave and exploit. Khalid's prices were fair, and the women were plentiful and beautiful.

Khalid issued an order to a minion who was standing at the bottom of the stairs. While he rushed away, the slave dealer walked the line of women to see his new stock in trade. He took his time, examining each woman in detail. He measured their breasts with his hands, pulling on and teasing the teats to hardness. His hands descended their legs, feeling the tautness of their thighs, the firmness of their calves. The women were forced to spread their legs so that he could fondle their sexes, manipulating them into wetness. Each woman was turned around and their buttocks and back inspected. Finally, the silver tape was ripped off of their mouths and the state of their teeth and gums examined.

Maddy's knees were shaking and sweat was pouring down her sides as she waited her turn. A small crowd of t-shirted and unkempt men had gathered and watched appreciatively as each girl was put through her paces.

Whatever was to be her fate, Maddy knew that this fat, callous man would have a large say in it.

When Khalid stood in front of Maddy, he made a comment to one of the bodyguards who had accompanied him down the stairs. The bodyguard nodded appreciatively. Maddy stood at least half a head taller than the other women. She was not lithe and demure of form as they were. Khalid reached his hands out and felt the muscles of Maddy's shoulders and arms. He seemed satisfied at what he found. Maddy could smell his foul, garlic laden breath as he held her face with his hand and peered into her starry blue eyes. She was revolted to be at this man's mercy. Dismal fear swept through her. She was caught up in a terrible nightmare from which she could not awaken. It was all too impossible to be true, that she would have been kidnapped and taken to some foreign land to be a sexual slave. All of her hopes and dreams of what life would bring her were dashed. "How will I ever bear it?" she thought to herself, miserably.

Khalid stroked Maddy's ample breasts admiringly. He put his lips to a nipple and sucked at it gently, flicking at it with his tongue. His hand had crept between Maddy's thighs and was prying apart her nether lips. Maddy could sense all of the men watching her, awaiting a demonstration of her feminine passion. She gritted her teeth, closed her eyes. The mouth on her breast and the hand in her loins began to enflame her. Her labia began to engorge with blood and her nipples became taut and hard. She could sense the softening and moistening of her sex as the hand expertly caressed her. None of the surrounding men spoke as they watched. The only sound was Maddy's rapidly quickening breath. When she could hold back no longer, she moaned.

A round of appreciative male cheers went up around the women. Khalid stepped back and held up his glistening hand to the crowd of lust filled men. Maddy, her knees weak from her passionate swoon, reddened. Tears flowed from her eyes. Khalid turned back to her and patted her on the cheek, mumbling some incomprehensible, consoling words to her. He tore off the tape that covered her mouth and finished his inspection.

While Khalid was inspecting his goods, two men were installing a wooden post in a hole about thirty feet in front of the women. It had an arm that stuck out like a gibbet. When Khalid was finished his tour, he stepped back and a path was cleared away by the surrounding men so that the women all had a clear view of the wooden post. Khalid went back down the line of nine frightened women. He paused at each one, searching their faces. When he was done, he came back again. He stopped at a small redhead who was standing next to Maddy. He pointed to her and barked a command to his men.

The redhead was dragged over to the post. Her hands were untied from behind her back and retied in front of her. She was crying and her eyes were wide with fear. A long, leather strap was tied to her wrists and passed through a ring in the arm that stuck out from the top of the thick post. The woman's hands were drawn high above her until she stood on her toes. Her ankles were tied together.

The tape that had covered the women's mouths had not been replaced after Khalid's inspection, and, as the purpose of being singled out occurred to the young woman, she began to beg and plead. "Oh, god, please don't hurt me, please! I'll do anything you say! Please, oh please, I don't want to be whipped! Oh, please don't do this, please!" Tears flowed freely down her anguished face. A man handed Khalid a many tasseled, leather whip. When the redheaded woman saw it, she moaned.

Maddy had seen poor Maureen whipped when she was a prisoner of Herman and Louise, but those whippings had been part of a deviant display of lust. This whipping, it appeared, was to be a cold, calculating demonstration of power.

Khalid shook the whip out to its full length. The redheaded girl closed her eyes and stiffened her body. There was absolute silence in the courtyard. Khalid raised his arm back and slung it forwards. The lashes of the whip struck the women's body across the legs, the stomach and the breasts. Her body recoiled from the blow, causing it to sway. She let out a piteous scream. Khalid reared back and struck the girl's body again. Again she screamed, even louder now. She had recommenced her pleading. "Ohhhhhhhhhhhhhhh! Please stop, please!"

The whip descended once more. Everywhere it landed there arose lines of bright red. Khalid moved so that he would have a clear shot at the crying and sobbing woman's back. She stiffened and screamed again as the lashes tore across her buttocks and thighs. "Ohhhhhhh! Ohhhhhhhhhhhhh! Ohhhhhhhhhhhhhhhhhh!" she cried. The young woman twisted and turned, desperately seeking to avoid the vicious tongues of the whip. She yelled frantically as the whip struck her three more times.

Finally, Khalid was done. The red headed woman's naked body was crisscrossed with the marks of the whip. She hung listlessly, moaning and crying.

The line of naked young women who had witnessed the demonstration of Khalid's authority and cruelty were aghast. Tears of fear and despair poured down more than one face. Khalid turned to them and smiled. "On your knees!" he yelled. The women hurried to obey him.

Apparently, this was a signal to the men because they began to approach the line of kneeling women. There were about twenty men in the courtyard and they queued up in front of the women. The first man in each line undid his pants and pulled out his cock. The women needed no explanation of what was expected.

Khalid stepped over to where Maddy was kneeling. He pushed the man in front of her aside, saying something to him harshly. He pulled Maddy to her feet.

"No cocksucking for you today," he said in a rough, deep voice. He signaled to one of the other men who handed him a roll of duct tape. He tore off a piece and placed it over Maddy's mouth. "Maybe tomorrow," he said to her laughing.

Although grateful that she did not have to suck the cocks of these strange men, Maddy was confused. Why was she being treated differently than the others, she thought to herself. What could it mean?

Khalid was in no mood to explain. The redheaded woman had been released from the post and her hands retied behind her back. A leash was affixed to her collar. One of the men handed it to Khalid. Without ado, Khalid turned and began his slow, ponderous walk back towards the building from whence he had come. The redheaded woman followed dolefully, close behind him.

Maddy was left standing naked in the sun while the other women worked to satisfy the crowd of men. She could see their mouths working energetically to fulfill their tasks. She could hear some of the women choke and cough as the men forced their cocks into their throats. Some of the men moaned when they came, others called out. Some just quietly accepted the flow of pleasure through their bodies as they unloaded their spunk into an obedient mouth.

It took more than an hour for all of the men to be satisfied. Undoubtedly, some of the men were serviced more than once. There was no clearer way to demonstrate to the naked and bound women their new purpose in life.

For the rest of the afternoon, the women knelt there. The men resumed their activities. Occasionally one of them would walk up and down the line weighing which woman's mouth to use. When chosen, the woman would dutifully and energetically fulfill her function.

As the light began to dim, and twilight approached, there came a clamor from one of the buildings. Whistles blew and a door slammed open. A line of naked women came streaming out. The leader began to run around the perimeter of the courtyard. Her wrists were bound behind her back.

All kinds of women, all shapes and sizes, blondes, brunettes, red heads, followed in a long line. There were about twenty five women in all. They ran after one another hurriedly, their breasts bouncing and swaying as they strained to follow the leader's pace. All of them had their hands tied behind their backs and all wore steel collars. Men chased them with small leather quirts, encouraging them to greater speed. They were all gagged.

The line of women circled the vast courtyard four times. Occasionally, one of the women would fall, only to be pounced upon by a whip wielding, t-shirted man. She would struggle to her feet, as quickly as she could, and rejoin the streaming line of naked, frightened women. When they were done, after the fourth pass, the exhausted women came to a halt and stood there panting and gasping for breath. After a few moments, the whistle blew again and they hustled back into the building.

It was almost dark when the line of kneeling women was commanded to stand and to walk towards the door from which the line of running women had come. One of the men tore the tape off of Maddy's mouth. It ripped her skin and stung terribly. The women were led into a huge bathroom with a long trough that served as a sink and a row of toilets against the wall. The women's hands were released and they were given to understand that they should clean themselves up and take care of their needs.

Several men stood and watched as the women relieved themselves and then rushed to the sink to wash. No talking was allowed. There were several bottles of green mouthwash on the shelf over the trough and the women made good use of it, washing the taste of their afternoon repast from their mouths. They also drank the cold, refreshing water to their hearts' content.

When the women were finished, their hands were rebound behind their backs and they were led, single file, out of the bathroom. They entered a long room lined with stalls on either side. In each stall was a bound and gagged, naked woman. A chain led from the back of each woman's collar to a ring in the wall.

The column of women was led towards the far side of the building. About three quarters of the way down, they came upon empty stalls. One by one, the women were led into a stall, a gag shoved roughly into their mouths and a chain connected from their collars to the wall.

Maddy received her gag with meek despair. She discovered that there was a worn, cotton pallet that lay along one side wall of her stall and a bench along the outer wall of the building. The chain was just long enough for her to stand a foot away from the entrance to her stall, which was about seven or eight feet deep. She saw a young woman across the way from her, naked and bound as she was. Their eyes met, and Maddy saw in the other girl's face the fierce sadness that she was herself experiencing. Now that the men had completed their task, there was no sound in the building except for the tinkling of chains and the muffled sobs of forlorn women. A wave of hopelessness washed over Maddy. She sat down on the bench and cried.

CHAPTER EIGHT

Martinez had had a hit. He had checked out the electronics store in the area where the Raytheon receiver had been sold. It was a small store, seemingly overloaded with inventory. It was in a small strip mall containing a 24 hour convenience store, a donut shop and a hairdresser's. The electronics store was sandwiched between the hairdressing salon and the donut shop.

The clerk who was behind the counter when Martinez came in was a short, balding man, about thirty-five. His hair was thinning and he wore thick, wire rimmed glasses. Martinez was not surprised to see the pocket protector and a row of pens in his shirt pocket.

The man was actually the owner and his knowledge about his stock in trade was encyclopedic.

"Sure," he said. "I remember selling that part. It was about three months back."

Martinez was surprised at the fellow's amiability. He thought all of these nerdish guys were like Irving, pointy headed wise asses. "Do you remember the guy who bought it?

"Absolutely. He bought two last year."

"Really?" Martinez said stupidly.

"Nah, I'm just telling you that for fun," the man said.

"Maybe I was right the first time," Martinez thought. He ignored the jibe. "It would mean a lot to some friends of mine to get a good description of the guy who bought those things," Martinez told the clerk. "If it's straight dope, there'll be a reward."

"Reward, scheward," the man said caustically.

Martinez explained about the suspected kidnapping and the believed involvement of the Raytheon receiver.

"Jeeze," the counterman said. "Hey, I'm sorry for giving you a hard time. I didn't know. Sure, I can give you a description of the guy."

"How come you remember this guy so good" Martinez asked.

"Well, when he first came in I thought he was one of those model airplane guys. This is the cream of receivers, and guys with big planes, real diehards, usually use them. I get a couple a year. But when I asked this guy what kind of plane he was flying he looked at me like I was a jerk and told me to mind my own fuckin' business. So I took his picture."

"You what?"

"I took his picture. See that camera up there?" The clerk pointed out a small hole in the wall above him. "I control it from down here." He pointed to a switch under the counter. "I take a picture of people I think are assholes. This way I can remember them if they ever come in again and ask for a favor. Here, take a look."

Martinez came around the counter. On the wall, out of the view of customers was a vast array of photographs.

"That's the guy, right there," the clerk said.

That was four days ago. Jake had copies of the photo made for everybody and the search began along the ten mile strip of the Callamuchie River for the man in the photo. Jake didn't want to spook the guy, so they had to be discrete about it. They would just have to carefully monitor all the local stores and gas stations until the guy came in. There was still some uncertainty in Jake's mind. There was still the possibility that the mud that had defined their search area had been picked up by some other guy while he was traveling through the area who had bought a receiver somewhere else. But it was the only real lead that they had.

It was Martinez who spotted him. Herman had been out scouting talent and was coming home after a long day on the road. He had stayed in the Tallahassee area for about a week and had some good leads. He stopped at the Duck and Run for some cigarettes and a six pack before he arrived home. Martinez had pulled into the single store parking lot for about the twentieth time in four days. He made Herman as he was walking out of the store.

Martinez pushed the button on his intercom phone. Jake picked up. "I've got him," Martinez told him.

"Are you sure," Jake asked.

"As if it was my own brother," Martinez answered.

"Don't lose him," Jake instructed.

"Fuck you," Martinez answered, miffed by his employer's lack of faith.

So, when Herman pulled his battered, old, green pick up from the parking lot of the Duck and Run, Martinez eased his rented Lumina behind him. There was only one main road and Martinez was able to keep a good distance between himself and Herman's pickup. About three miles down the road, Martinez saw the truck make a left into a weed obscured, dirt driveway. "Bingo!" he said.

* * * * * * * * * * *

Maddy had cried herself out by the time one of the men came by to feed her dinner. He was pushing a large cart down the center aisle of the building, stopping at each stall, ladling out a bowl of stew. When he came to Maddy, he undid her gag, and, toying with one of her breasts, said, "No talk. Eat."

Maddy understood very well what the man meant. She had nothing to say to any other of the miserable women there anyway. What could she tell them that would allay their fears, and what could they tell her? She didn't want to know what her fate would be. It was hard enough to deal with her present, never mind her future.

She had believed that the man would untie her hands from behind her back to eat, but this was not to be. He merely placed the bowl of stew on the floor just inside the entrance to her stall. When Maddy looked up at him, dismayed, he just smiled.

Maddy was in no mood to equivocate. She was famished. And she knew that her despair was worsened by being hungry and tired. Also, who knew when the next chance to eat would be? Due to her long legs and tall frame, it was a difficult maneuver for Maddy to lower her face sufficiently to eat out of the bowl without tipping over. She had to spread her legs as wide as they would go. As she did so, she looked up and saw the girl in the stall opposite hers, a small blonde girl with tiny, pointed breasts, with her face buried in her bowl. As the girl came up for air to chew, she saw Maddy looking over at her. She looked forlornly at Maddy, ashamed of her debasement. Maddy gave her a look of commiseration and lowered her own mouth to the bowl.

It was only a few minutes later that the man came back with the cart. Maddy was finishing the last vestiges of the stew. Lamb, she thought it was, spicy and fatty. There were a few soggy carrots and some potatoes too. The man picked up the bowl and threw it on the cart. He had a wet cloth and he used it to wash Maddy's face. She had just swallowed the last mouthful when he jammed the gag back into her mouth.

Shortly after the food man had left, a somewhat more well dressed, middle aged man appeared. He had a dark face, eyes that were almost black. He sported a long, thick, black moustache. He was fit, hard. He stepped into the stall and Maddy shrank away from him. She had been sitting on the bench, naked, her arms still tied behind her, trying to block out all thoughts about what tomorrow would bring. When the man entered, she retreated to the corner. As he stepped closer, she began to tremble.

"Stand up!" the man ordered.

Frightened, Maddy slowly rose to her feet. The man pulled her to the middle of the stall, directly under the dimly lit bulb which was overhead. His eyes flowed over Maddy's breasts and belly, knowingly. He circled her breasts with his hands, flicking the nipples with his thumbs. In spite of herself, Maddy felt her nipples tighten. There was a heavy expectancy in her loins. The man smiled. He took from his pocket a long piece of red cloth. He knotted its end on the ring at the front of Maddy's collar. He patted her on the head.

"No fucking tonight," he said, amused. The man then turned and left Maddy's stall only to cross over to the stall of the petit blond girl across the way. She was sitting on her bench and she, too, rose when the man entered. At first, the man paid her no mind. He stripped off his black t-shirt to reveal his taut, muscled chest. Then he removed his shoes and pants.

The blond girl seemed to have no doubt as to what was in store for her. Maddy saw her face cringe as she tried to hide in the corner of the stall. When the man had completed disrobing, he grabbed the chain that led to the girl's collar and reigned her in. When she resisted, his hand flashed out like lightening, striking her twice across the breasts. Maddy heard the girl's muffled cry.

Maddy watched as the man forced the blond girl to bend over and rest her forehead on the bench. He kicked her legs apart so that her sex was available to him. He ran his hand over the girl's buttocks and then between her legs. Maddy watched as he manipulated her sex. She knew that the blond girl was about to be raped. It was like watching a train wreck. She was repelled by what she saw, but she could not turn her eyes away.

When the man was satisfied that the blond girl was sufficiently lubricated, he placed his body behind her. His bulk made the girl's body all but disappear. The girl moaned through her gag as the man thrust his cock home. The man began to rock into her, his hands on her hips. While he was fucking the blond girl, two more men came by and stopped at the stall to watch. Like most of the men there, they were unkempt and bearded. They exchanged words and laughed as they watched the buttocks of the girl's assailant pound at her flesh. The man let out a loud groan as he came. When he was done, he backed away from the girl. The two other men began to undress to take advantage of the already primed victim.

All through the night, Maddy could hear the ongoing assaults throughout the barracks-like building. She could hear women moaning and crying, the sound of men taking their pleasure. Once or twice she heard the plea of a recalcitrant young woman followed by the sound of flesh striking flesh. There would be a cry and then the sound of a woman moaning. Twice, men came into Maddy's cell only to be disappointed by the red flag she wore attached to her collar. The flag may have spared her from being raped, but it did not spare her from the molestations of the men as they sampled her inviting breasts or stroked her sex into responsiveness.

The young woman was happy to be spared an invasion of her body, but she was frightened at what it meant. Why was she being singled out? Why was she being treated differently than all the other women? She lay on her pallet and tried to suppress the noises of the callous and casual rapes going on all around her. Eventually, the activity died down and Maddy was able to find fitful sleep on her thin, cotton bedding.

She was awoken by the shrill call of whistles being blown. Faint sunlight was coming in through the small window high on the outer wall of her stall. It was morning. She saw two men walk past, shiny, steel whistles in their mouths. Although she did not know what routine she was expected to follow, she guessed that at the very least, she was required to be up and on her feet. She took a few moments to use the bucket in the corner to relieve herself. The men with the whistles returned. One of them had a long cane and he pointed to the floor just inside Maddy's stall and barked strange, harsh words at her. She took this to mean that she was to stand by the entrance to her stall and await developments.

A few moments later, one of the men came in and released her collar from its chain, removing the red cloth. She was pulled into the hallway where she saw the other women lining up. When all of the women were outside of their stalls, the line began to move forwards. When she got close to the other end of the long building, she could see that the women were being led out into the courtyard. Once outside, she saw that the sun had not yet fully risen. There was still a sharp chill in the air. The women, about thirty five of them in all now, were snaked around the courtyard. When the last woman was outside, another whistle blew and the leader began to run, each woman following in her turn. When the woman in front of Maddy started to run, Maddy followed her unquestioningly.

Thirty five naked women, gagged and hands tied behind their backs, sprinted around the circumference of the courtyard. Puffs of cloudy vapor steamed out of their noses as if they were dragons. The cobblestones were cold and wet from a light rain during the night. They were slippery, and more than one woman went down, bouncing and skidding on the stones. A man would be on her immediately, lashing at her with a whip until she rose to her feet and began to run again.

Maddy considered herself in good shape, but it was difficult to draw enough air through her nose to stop from hyperventilating. Her chest felt like to burst as the line completed lap after lap. Men were standing around drinking coffee from steaming mugs, laughing and jesting at the display of naked breasts bobbing and weaving as the women fearfully kept up the punishing pace. Maddy lost count of the laps, but finally the whistle blew and the leaders of the line of women slowed down and came to a stop.

Maddy's muscles ached and she was straining to catch her breath. Many of the women doubled over, and some fell to their knees. The men patiently waited while the women recovered from their exertions. After some time, the whistles blew again and the line was escorted to a door in one of the other buildings. The door led to a huge bathroom with showerheads along one wall and sinks and toilets along the other. As each woman entered, her gag and bindings were removed. There were ten shower heads and the women took quick turns wetting their bodies and rubbing themselves down with soap. There was shampoo for their hair and large, coarse towels to dry off with. On the sinks were tooth and hair brushes.

All the while in the bathroom, the women were urged along by the yelling and shouting of the men. The women hurriedly, but silently, performed their ablutions. Maddy was grateful to use the toilet. She was brushing out her long, brown hair when the whistles sounded again. The women lined up obediently and were marched outside and back into the barracks. As they entered the building, their gags were reaffixed and their hands rebound behind their backs.

There seemed to be no special order for the women, and Maddy found herself in a different stall from before. Opposite her was a shapely, tall, brunette girl, with shoulder length hair. Maddy followed the woman's example and stood at her stall's entrance. Her collar had been rechained to the wall. The food cart came by and Maddy was forced to eat from the floor as before. After the bowls were collected and her gag reinstalled, Maddy forlornly resumed her perch on the wooden bench. She heard the door to the barracks slam shut and then an almost ghostly silence, the silence of gagged and helpless women.

CHAPTER NINE

Jake had turned his room in the local Motel Six into a war room. There were aerial shots of the small, downtrodden house and barn. Surveillance gear was strewn around the room. A large map of the area was pinned to the wall. Tucker, Martinez and the new arrivals, Leon and Curley, were sitting around the room awaiting instructions.

They had been watching the little dirt road off of Route 286 for three days. The green pickup had come out two or three times during that period. It was too risky to tail it all the time, so Jake had a beeper installed under the bumper when the truck stopped at the local Piggly Wiggly. Earlier that day, a van had pulled out of the small road and headed south. The man was driving and an older woman sat in the passenger's seat. Martinez followed them as far as the Interstate and gave up the chase.

"We need to know when they're coming back," Jake said. "I want to case the farmhouse and barn from top to bottom."

Leon, a slim, boney kind of guy, tall with a mop of curly brown hair, spoke up. "Let Curley and me sit at the Interstate and watch for them coming back."

"What makes you think that they'll come back the same way?" asked Jake. "If they're doing what we think they're doing, they will probably be too careful to take the same route all the time."

"There's only two ways into the farmhouse driveway," Martinez offered. "They have to come either north or south on 286. We could station a lookout at each end, a couple of miles away."

"Okay," Jake agreed. "Martinez and Tucker, you take the north end. What's the nearest crossroads?"

"Dawes Road," answered Martinez. "It's about five miles up."

"Shit," Jake cursed. "That'll give me all of about ten minutes warning when they come back." He paused, thinking. "That'll have to do. But you guys'll have to stay awake and alert. I don't want them to come rolling in when I'm checking out the basement."

"Don't worry, Jake. We'll take care of it," Martinez answered.

"The Interstate is about 15 miles south of the driveway. At least there I'll have a little more warning," Jake observed. He looked at his watch. It was 2 P.M. "I don't want to wait until dark. I might miss something." To Martinez he said, "Drop me off now. Come back around 6. I'll be done by then."

The meeting broke up and the men moved on to their tasks. It was decided that Irving would accompany Jake since he had the best eye for detail. Martinez pulled the car over about 30 feet from the entrance to the driveway and Jake and Irving got out. They waited until they were sure no cars were coming in either direction and they dove into the woods. Martinez and Tucker left to take up their post.

Jake and Irving walked carefully through the woods. Although the man had left with a woman, there still might be someone at the house. Jake did not want to be discovered prematurely. He would close in when he knew what was what.

It took the men about twenty minutes to creep the mile or so through the woods up to the house. At the edge of the woods, Jake lay down and eyed the building with a small pair of binoculars. He would look and wait at least a half hour before moving in. Hopefully, if there was someone there, they would make themselves known during that time period.

Having seen no movement, Jake nudged Irving and the two men crept slowly towards the house. Jake had his Beretta out. Irving carried a small .38. Silently, Jake climbed the porch and peered in the window. Still nothing. He opened the screen door carefully and tested the front door. It was locked. He motioned Irving to circle the building to the left and he took off to the right. They met at the back of the house. The back door was also locked, but Jake felt more comfortable jimmying the lock back there where, if a car pulled up, they wouldn't be seen.

The door sprung open and the men tiptoed inside. The first order of business was making sure that the house was indeed empty. Quickly and efficiently, the men searched all of the rooms. When they were satisfied, they began to look around in earnest.

Irving made the first important discovery. In a chest in the bedroom, he found a pile of chains and handcuffs. There were several leather gags and hoods. He showed them to Jake. "Looks like we've come to the right place," he said.

Jake nodded. Under a floorboard in a closet in the back hall, he found several bankbooks, all from banks outside of the country. They amounted all together over two million dollars. "A nice little nest egg," he thought. "Who would live in a shithole like this if they had $2 million dollars?"

Irving called out to Jake, who was searching the living room. In the larder, off the kitchen, there were several cases of franks and beans. "So?" Jake commented when Irving showed them to him.

"So, if you had to keep someone prisoner for a while and you didn't want to cook for them, what would you feed them? Caviar?"

"Maybe they just like franks and beans?" Jake said.

"Right. Enough to store four cases of them in the event of emergency?"

"Okay," Jake conceded. "But there has to be a place to keep the prisoner or prisoners around here somewhere. I checked the basement, there's nothing there. That leaves the barn. I'm going to check it out. There's a computer in the living room. See what you can find."

Jake scurried to the barn, careful not to leave any tracks. It was padlocked shut. It was a conventional three tumbler Master combination lock. Jake had the lock undone within a minute. He swung the door open and went inside. The barn was as decrepit as the house. There were no storerooms that could serve as a jail. Jake looked around, perplexed. "There's got to be a lockup here somewhere."

He decided to check around outside. He started at the perimeter of the barn and then worked himself around in a widening circle. When he got to the edge of the trees, on the opposite side of the property from the road, he saw two pipes sticking up from the ground. Curious, he leaned over and put his hand over one. He felt a push of air. He put his hand over the other one and there was a slight suction. When he put his ear to one pipe he could hear the sound of a small fan whirring. Something was underground.

There was no obvious entry outside, so it had to be in the barn. He returned inside and made another examination of its contents, more carefully this time. He noted a small pile of wooden skids near the far side of the barn. There were scrape marks on the floor as if they had been moved. He picked them up carefully, first noting their exact position, and saw underneath them a small trapdoor. It had a sturdy brass lock on it. This was what he was looking for.

Not fifteen feet below where Jake stood, Maureen and a small, brunette girl were locked in their cages. Louise had come to them about two hours before and washed and fed them. Louise figured that they were good for at least 48 hours, probably more. She saw Maureen cringing in her cage and wished that she had time for a good cuntlicking before she and Herman left for Florida. "We'll be back in a couple of days, slut," she told the unhappy girl. "Don't go anywhere." Louise laughed at her own joke. She poked the electric wand into Maureen's cage and gave her a jolt. Maureen moaned and spasmed at the pain. The brunette girl watched, wide-eyed. As Louise pushed the wand into her cage, she tried to back away from it, putting her back against the rear of the cage. Louise gave her a jolt too. The brunette girl squealed and cried out, her protestations frustrated by the thick leather gag in her mouth. "You be a good girl too!" Louise told her.

The caged young women watched as Louise mounted the stairs. The trapdoor slammed shut with a loud thud. They could hear the click of the bolt being locked into place.

Due to the heavy insulation of the 'hole', neither Jake nor the young women below knew that they were in close proximity to each other. Jake yearned to learn what was under the trapdoor, but didn't want to fuck with the lock. Something was down there all right. He would find out when he sprung his trap on the old couple.

Back in the house, Irving had struck gold. The computer contained a detailed record of all of the transactions of the couple over the last four years. It had been locked in a coded file that was no match for Irving's ingenuity. The girls were listed by first name. Maddy's was among the last group. Jake saw her price of $50,000 next to Maddy's name. She was a good looking girl, all right, but why was her price so much more than the others? There was only one other price that broke $40,000.

"Is there any information on who they were sold to?" Jake asked Irving.

"Just the notation, 'Elizabeth'," Irving replied.

"I found the hiding place. It's under the barn."

"Is there anybody in it?" Irving asked.

"Don't know," Jake replied. "I didn't want to fuck with the lock."

"But if there are any girls down there we've got to get them out!" Irving said frantically.

"Hold your horses, Irving," Jake answered harshly. "We've got one goal on this job and one only. That's to find Maddy and bring her back from wherever they've taken her. I'm not concerned with any other damsels in distress, got it!"

"You can't mean that!" Irving insisted. "You're going to let these girls be sold into slavery?"

"We don't even know if there are any girls down there," Jake insisted. "You're on my team and you're going to follow my orders. Got that?"

Irving blanched. Jake was not one to fuck around with. "Okay, Jake. If that's what you say."

"That's what I say. Now we're going to set up surveillance on this place and we'll move when I decide."

The men restored the computer and the locks to how they found them and left the house. Irving set up tiny, remote controlled, battery operated cameras around the perimeter and in the barn from the backpack that he had carried in. When the job was finished, the men retreated though the woods back to the road. They called Martinez who picked them up.

* * * * * * * * * * *

Maddy sat on her bench listlessly. The morning had drifted on uneventfully. The brown haired girl in the opposite stall stared back at her whenever she looked up. Occasionally, she could hear the rattling of a chain as one or another of the girls changed positions.

Maddy heard the barracks door open and the heavy tread of boots on the wooden floor. As the sound came closer, she felt a sinking in her stomach. The presence of the men boded only ill to someone. She prayed that it wasn't her.

Just then two men appeared at the entrance to her stall. One of them was carrying a leash. Maddy moaned in fear. Whatever the reason she had been held back and treated differently from the other women was, she felt, about to be revealed. One of the men ordered her to her feet. While he disconnected her chain from her collar, the other man attached the leash. She felt a tug on her neck and was propelled forwards.

Maddy was led past the open stalls of the other women. She had time only to glance at the naked and gagged females as she was trundled by. Each one looked up as she passed, silent witnesses to her departure.

The men led Maddy through the barracks door out to the courtyard. The sun was bright and it was a warm and beautiful day. As before, men seemed to be engaged in random activities throughout. One of the Mercedes had just been started up and coasted up to the gate. Maddy saw the gate swing open and the car, filled with male passengers, drive through it and away.

She was taken to a doorway at the far right end of the building opposite the barracks. She was led through an outer room which contained a desk and a man sitting behind it. At the end of a long hallway, the man who was leading her opened a door and pulled her into a small room with an elevated chair in the middle of it.

Maddy's hands were unbound and she was pushed into the chair. Her wrists were locked into the arms of the chair and her ankles strapped to its legs. One of the men removed her gag, unbuckling it from the back of her head. Maddy yearned desperately to learn why she had been brought here but was too afraid to make any sound.

The chair was straight-backed, and Maddy sat at full attention. One of the men removed the steel collar that had been around her neck and replaced it with a wide one made of leather. The collar was wider in front than in the back and forced Maddy to raise her head. A bracket was attached to the arms of the chair. It had an adjustable arm in the middle which the men raised to the level of Maddy's mouth. At the end of the arm was a thick leather plug. One of the men held Maddy's head still while the plug was presented to her lips. Maddy resisted the opening of her mouth. She did not know the reason for this bizarre apparatus, but it did not bode well for her. She tried to speak, to beg the men not to force the plug into her mouth. The man holding her head released it and stepped back. For one moment, Maddy thought that she had won, that she would be spared. But the man gave her a single jab to her solar plexus. The air rushed out of her lungs. She opened her mouth in a desperate effort to draw in oxygen. At her second breath, the leather plug was jammed in.

While Maddy strained to breathe in through her nose, the men finished the adjustments to the apparatus. There was a clamping device that was adjusted to the contours of her chin and pressed in tight. The gag had a pump on its end and, after the men filled it full of air, the gag filled the cavity of Maddy's mouth tightly. The net effect was to fix Maddy's head in a static position. She could not move her head up or down, backwards or forwards or side to side. Tight straps around her torso completed her immobility. One of the men squeezed her breast, rubbing his other hand in her long, strait, auburn hair and smiling. He shut the door behind them as they left.

The frightened girl sat alone in the room for a long time. She gave up straining at her bonds almost immediately. But she could not help the writhing of her hands or the tremors in her legs. Tears flowed down her face as she tried not to imagine what strange torture she was about to undergo.

At last, the door to the room opened. A heavy set, middle aged, peasant woman entered. She had blond hair that was tied up in a bright yellow kerchief on her head. Her face was broad and friendly. She wore a plain, brown skirt and a white top embroidered with yellow and pink flowers across the bodice. She smiled at Maddy as she entered and spoke words of greeting. She was carrying a large basket over one arm and a large, covered, steel bowl that had steam leaking from its sides. The woman walked behind Maddy and the girl could hear her put the bowl and basket down on a narrow table that stood against the wall.

The woman came around to the front of Maddy and studied her. Smiling, she stroked the frightened girl's cheek as if to calm her. Maddy took some small comfort at the seemingly benign nature of the woman. She pleaded with her with her eyes. The woman's blue eyes seemed gentle, kind. Maybe she would help her.

Without further ado, the woman retreated back around Maddy. Maddy heard her rummaging around in her basket and then felt the woman's hands on her head. She felt the bristles of a brush run through her hair. Maddy tried to talk to the woman, desperate to gain some aid and sympathy from her. Her words were just mumbled sounds, however, and the woman paid them no mind.

After the woman had thoroughly brushed Maddy's long, reddish brown hair, Maddy felt the woman pull her hair back. The woman was twisting her hair into a long pony tail. Maddy felt that it was odd that the woman was only using the hair at the back of her head. Maddy felt a rubber band rolled up against her head, pulling the hairs close to her head tight. More bands were attached to the conjoined hair, down its length.

There was a moment's silence as the woman went back to her basket. Then Maddy heard the unmistakable sound of scissors. Realizing that her hair was to be cut, Maddy tried to struggle out of her chair. She desperately tried to move her head to frustrate the clipping of her locks. But she was held tight and the most movement that she could effect was a slight tremor in her torso.

Maddy could not see what the woman was doing, but she could feel and see the locks of her hair falling away at the front and sides. The woman expertly began to remove all of her hair except that which had been rolled together in the back. The hissing of the scissors was torture to Maddy as her precious growth was sliced away. When the woman was finished with the scissors, Maddy could feel the nakedness of her head. She cried as she imagined her new, strange appearance. The woman ran her hand over the stubble left in the areas that had been cut. Maddy felt the woman's heavy, calloused hand pat her cheek from behind and heard her say something in her thick, harshly accented native language.

Just when she thought that the woman was finished, Maddy heard the rumbling of a small cart being rolled up to the back of the chair. She heard the top lifted off of the steel bowl and it being placed down on the cart behind her.

There was the sound of a brush being whisked in a bowl and then Maddy felt the application of warm, foamy soap to her head. The girl tried to scream when she realized that her head was to be shaved. From an appearance point of view, it really didn't matter since the damage had already been done. But it was the indignity of it all that caused Maddy to revolt with all her being. She was being turned into some kind of freak!

The blond, gleeful, peasant woman paid no attention to Maddy's demonstration as she went about her task of removing the stubble from the helpless girl's head. She hummed a little song while she used a finely honed, strait razor to remove the stubble down to its very roots. When she was done, she washed Maddy's head free of the remnants of the soap. She ran her hands over the smooth cranium, rubbing in a soothing cream. Maddy was not in a position to appreciate the gesture as she was overwhelmed with shame and despair. These people had control of her body. Nothing was left to her. "What do I look like? What more will they do to me?" she wondered, fearfully.

Maddy felt the woman begin to brush the remnants of her hair from her naked body. She was using a small whisk broom and the stiff bristles scratched her skin. The woman brushed the hair onto the floor. When she was satisfied that all of the hair was brushed off, she grabbed another broom and swept up all of the droppings. The hair was brushed into a dustpan and then poured into a plastic bag.

To Maddy's dismay, there was one more indignity. The blond woman came around in front of her and began to toy with her breasts. She smiled as she gently pinched and massaged them. She said something sweetly in her native patois, something incongruous to the terrible deed she had just performed on the young woman. When she tired of her assault on Maddy's heavy, round, feminine mounds, she stood back and took in the results of her work. She smiled at the unhappy young woman's forlorn face, satisfied.

The blond, peasant woman gathered up her things and headed for the door. She balanced the steel bowl in one arm and draped the handle to the basket over the other. She looked back at Maddy's tear streaked face once more before she left. "Goodbye," she said in heavily accented English, and she was gone.

Maddy sat in the chair stunned at what had happened to her. She could not understand its meaning. Why would someone want to make her look so strange?

After about a half hour, the men returned. They removed Maddy from the chair. Grabbing her by the arms, they dragged her from the room and further down the hallway. Maddy was too shocked to speak. They entered another room where an older man with wire rimmed glasses waited for them. He wore a leather apron around his waist and a thick denim work shirt. Behind him were shelves of leather straps and bindings. Maddy was spun around and she felt the man measuring the width of her shoulders and the length of her torso. After a moment or two, she felt the man reach around her from behind and drape a leather harness over her chest. A belt ran just under her breasts and was pulled tight and fastened behind her back. A leather strap ran up between her breasts and divided, one strap rising over each shoulder. The straps were attached to the belt.

Too afraid to struggle, Maddy passively allowed the man to adorn her body with the leather harness. She was still wearing the thick collar and could not lower her head to see what had been affixed to her. Her arms were pulled behind her and she felt leather bracelets being attached to her wrists. Her wrists were then raised behind her back and attached to the harness behind her by means of metal clips.

Maddy felt the strain on her shoulders as her wrists were forced up her back. Her moaning protests were ignored.

There was a pause while the man with the glasses returned to his shelves to retrieve more accouterments for Maddy's body. Her arms were held tightly by the two men who had brought her and she could not turn around to see what he was doing. She felt a tug at her pony tail and something being threaded up it. When it reached her head, it was pulled over the top and tugged down over her ears and her face. Momentarily, the young girl was in darkness as the leather hood covered her eyes. "Oh, please, no, please," Maddy cried. It was the first words she had been able to speak for days. Her terror at what was being done to her finally overcame her fear of the whip or whatever else these men could do to her.

Maddy struggled as the man adjusted the hood to her head, begging and pleading to be let go. It was if a dam inside her had broken. "Please don't do this to me, please!" she cried out. One of the men at her sides grabbed a nipple on her breast and twisted it harshly. Maddy moaned in pain. He barked a harsh word to her. She did not understand its meaning, but was able to gather its tenor. She stopped struggling and the pain in her breast stopped. She may have stopped screaming, but inside, she was begging and pleading with her maker to come to her aid.

When the hood was finally adjusted and strapped on, it covered her whole head and her face down to below her nose. The nostrils were left free. Only two narrow, vertical slits let in light for her eyes and her vision was consequently greatly diminished. She felt a long, thick leather covered bar pressed into her mouth and jammed in between her teeth. It spread her cheeks open widely. A sharp metal plate depressed her tongue. The strange gag was buckled tightly behind her head.

Once the men had placed heavy, black, high top boots on her feet, they stood around the frantic girl and admired their handiwork. A leash was affixed to her collar and she was led around the room while the men laughed and joked. Maddy's sounds of protest were oddly animalistic. A hand grabbed her sex and started to stroke her between the legs. Her legs were locked open by the men's legs and Maddy was unable to close them. A mouth began to suck on one of her breasts while a hand massaged the other. Maddy tried to resist the stoking of her passion. She tried to swing her torso free and only succeeded in adding to the men's merriment. Slowly, as her pussy moistened and engorged with blood, she felt heat rising in her loins. Fingers plunged inside her, stroking in and out, spreading her lubrication over her tender nether lips. A finger began to tease her button of pleasure, shooting a tingling throughout her body. Her breathing became heavy and she began to moan. She could no longer resist and she pressed her vulva against the hand that was tormenting her. When she came, her whole body shuddered. Her knees weakened and she fell back into the arms of the man behind her. Pulse after pulse of exquisite pleasure flowed through her. She could hear the men laughing as she came.

When they were satisfied that she was done, the men settled her back on her feet. She felt a slap on her behind as she was tugged forward by her leash. She followed the men helplessly back out into the courtyard.

Maddy was left to stand alone in the courtyard for a long time. Her collar was attached to a post by a ring in its back, high up, so she could not sit down or kneel. Her obscured vision made her feel more naked than before, if that were possible, probably because she could not see the men who she imagined were ogling her. A truck had pulled into the courtyard while she had been inside the building and she could see, dimly, several hooded and bound women being loaded into its canvass covered back. When the women were loaded, the truck pulled out.

Twice during the time she was standing there, Maddy heard the familiar whistles blowing. She heard the door to the barracks opening and was able to discern the naked women flowing out of it. She could see their outlines as they dashed around the courtyard and streamed past her. She could hear their ragged breathing and the slapping of their naked feet on the cobblestones. Once, her gag was removed and she was given water to drink. She was allowed to pee in a bucket.

It was late in the afternoon that Maddy heard the gate opening again and the motor of a truck entering. It was a large, dark blue, pickup truck and it was towing a tall, narrow, covered trailer behind it. There was a commotion in the courtyard and Maddy heard thick boots descending the stairs from the upper level of the building. Her collar was undone from the pole, a leash attached to the front, and she felt herself being pulled over toward the truck. She could only see bits and pieces of it at a time due to her narrowly constricted vision. It was obvious that the truck had come for her.

She was stopped a few feet away from it. She saw the outline of the driver as he approached her. Someone grabbed her cheeks and held her head still. She could see through the slit to her hood that it was the greasy fat man from the day before. She felt hands stroke her buttocks and test her thighs. Hands grabbed her breasts from behind and assessed them. Her pony tail was pulled sharply, causing her to utter a cry. Words were exchanged and Maddy saw two hands shaking.

There was a tug on her leash again and Maddy felt herself being drawn over to the trailer behind the truck.

She pulled back on the leash, terrified. She realized that she had been sold, had probably been sold long before she had even arrived at this god forsaken place. That was why she was treated differently than the other women, she was a special order! That could only mean that some special, terrible fate awaited her!

Strong hands grabbed Maddy's arms and she was forced towards the truck. Men were laughing and joking around her. Hands slapped her buttocks, stinging her. She felt herself lifted into the trailer. Her waist was pressed against a thick wooden beam and she was strapped to it. Her legs were spread and her boots buckled to the floor. A man brushed by her and affixed her leash to the front of the trailer. She felt the man duck back under the beam and stand behind her. His hand cupped her sex from behind. He whispered something she could not understand in her ear as he probed her loins. Maddy was frantic with fear. She pulled and tugged at her bonds and mindlessly begged for release. She tried to sway her hips to avoid the hand that was tormenting her. She had felt deeply ashamed and degraded when the men had forced her to orgasm earlier that day and she desperately wanted to avoid a repetition of that act. However, when the man was satisfied that she was lubricated and aroused, he withdrew his hand. Maddy could feel the wetness of her cleft and its distended lips. In spite of her shame, part of her yearned for release.

The trailer jolted slightly as the man stepped down off of it. A few moments later, Maddy heard the truck door slam and the engine turn over. The trailer began to move with a small jerk and Maddy's body swayed backwards, causing the leash from her collar to pull taut. She felt the trailer wheeled in a wide circle, straighten out and then speed up. When the rumbling of the tires over the cobblestones ceased, Maddy knew that she had left the courtyard and had passed through the gate.

The inside of the trailer was hot and dusty. There were vents in the front to facilitate the flow of air, and the back of the trailer was open. But the hot sun baked the top and sides of the trailer unmercifully. Maddy felt each bump in the road, as she was jostled back and forth. Her legs tired quickly and she alleviated the strain on them by leaning against the beam that was set against her waist. The bit-like gag in her mouth and the steel plate that depressed her tongue were constant reminders of her helplessness. When she moved her head, she could feel the long pony tail, the remnant of her once beautiful hair, brush across her back and her bound arms. Her spread legs made vulnerable her naked and gaping sex.

Even though the back of the trailer was open, Maddy could not see anything of the area through which they were passing. She could turn her head slightly, but the limited vision permitted by the slits in her hood prevented her from seeing behind her. She was conscious, though, of the fact that any vehicle driving behind the trailer would have a clear view of her naked buttocks and the fact that she was hooded and restrained. She could hear other vehicles passing them and once or twice she heard car horns honking behind her. It became evident to Maddy that her possessors had no concern that it be known that they were transporting an unwilling, bound and naked female.

After a few hours, the light in the trailer began to fade. The sun was setting and the heat in the trailer began to abate. Maddy's throat was parched. The truck continued on to its unknown destination. Maddy could see the reflection of the headlights of the cars behind them on the wall in front of her as well as the shadow of her bound form.

Eventually, the lights behind her diminished and she was cast in near total darkness.

Twice, the man pulled the truck and trailer to the side of the road. Each time, the man released Maddy from her bindings, led her from the van and let her pee. He unbuckled her cruel gag and let her drink. The only things that Maddy could see were the running lights of the trailer and, when she looked up, the star studded sky above. Once she was regagged, Maddy was returned to the trailer and the journey was resumed.

At one point, the truck pulled into a well lit service area. Maddy could see the bright fluorescent lights shining in through the vents of the trailer and could hear the sounds of the driver leaving the truck and of the truck being gassed. Men were talking outside. Desperately, Maddy tried to yell and scream through her gag. She used her weight to begin to rock the trailer in the furtive hope that some one would come to her aid. The voices moved to the back of the trailer. Maddy could hear the men talking right behind her. They were apparently amused at her vain efforts to seek aid. She heard them laugh. The door to the truck opened and closed and the trailer was once more set in motion. Maddy leaned against the beam across her waist and cried.

She was virtually asleep on her feet the next time that the truck slowed to a stop. She was jerked awake by the cessation of movement. It was still dark outside. She heard the truck door open and close and felt the trailer rock as the man stepped up into it. She could feel him testing her bindings. When he was satisfied, he patted her on the rump and stepped out of the van. Maddy could hear the sound of his boots on gravel as he walked away.

Maddy was left to herself, standing in the trailer, for the rest of the night. She slept fitfully. Every time that she fell into deep sleep, she was jolted awake by the sensation of falling. The air was cold and she shivered in the darkness of the trailer. She watched gratefully as the morning light began to filter in through the vents in front of her. She was tired and frightened. She could hear activity commencing around the trailer, the crowing of a rooster, the sound of feet on gravel. As the day grew brighter, several times she sensed the presence of persons behind her peering in.

Finally, someone came to release her. Her legs ached terribly and she needed desperately to pee again. She was thirsty and hungry too. The bright light of the day blinded her at first as she was led by her leash from the van. She only had a few moments to adjust when two pieces of black tape were applied to her hood, covering up the small slits that had been her narrow windows on the world. She stumbled as she was dragged forwards by unseen hands. The gravel was rough underfoot and she almost fell twice, as sharp rocks stuck into her boots. She felt the ground turn to packed earth, which made the going easier.

Maddy couldn't tell how far she had been dragged when she was finally brought to a halt. She felt her leash attached to a pole and heard her leader walk away. While she awaited the next development, she could hear the steadily increasing sounds of activity around her. People were passing to and fro. She heard the pounding of heavily shod feet and the crack of a whip. After about an hour, her leash was unfastened from the pole and her journey began anew. This time she was pulled over onto a patch of grass and forced to squat. She felt a great sense of relief as her bladder was emptied. She was pulled to her feet and a wet cloth rubbed over her sex, cleaning the last drops of urine away.

The next time that she was brought to a halt, her leader stood next to her holding her leash as if anticipating some event. She heard the clip clop of a horse's hoofs approach. The horse stopped and she heard the creaking of a leather saddle as apparently someone dismounted. A deep, smooth voice made some exclamation. The man who held her leash made a deferential sound and Maddy felt her head pushed forwards and down into a little bow. Hands assessed her shoulders, soft, but strong hands, male hands. They ran down her sides and measured her thighs. The deep, sonorous voice, issued sounds of satisfaction.

Next, Maddy felt the hands seize her breasts. A strange warmth went through her as they gently massaged her sensitive globes. Thumbs pressed on her nipples, stroking them until they stiffened. Maddy felt a face draw close to her and then lips seize the nipple of one breast. She started to struggle as she felt a hot tongue twirl around the rough, pink skin that surrounded the nipple. Strong, rough hands held her arms tightly and legs circled hers, forcing them open. A softer, knowledgeable hand caressed the outer lips of her sex lightly.

Maddy could hear and sense the presence of a small crowd of people around her. She groaned with shame as the hand traced the gap between her tingling labia and drew moisture from her. She felt her nether lips soften and distend as the finger entered her. She tried to beg the man to stop, but her voice emerged as a garbled whine. There was laughter all around.

At the command of the man with the deep, refined, almost aristocratic voice, Maddy felt herself dragged a short distance and pushed back onto what felt like a bale of hay. Her legs were lifted and spread apart. Hands held her down. The man placed himself between her legs and leaned over her. When she felt the fleshy end of a stiff cock press against her moist hole, Maddy began to convulse in physical protest. Her legs were gripped all the more tightly and her body was pressed more firmly against the bale of hay beneath her. Slowly, the hard, hot pole pushed itself inside. She felt it press her sheath open as it filled her. Her assailant had his weight upon her now as he sank deeper and deeper into her moist slit. When fully seated in her cunt, the prick began a remorseless rhythm, fucking her slowly, worrying the little nub at its apex, caressing its interior walls.

Although Maddy had known that sooner or later she would be raped, she nonetheless felt debased and ashamed now that it was actually happening. Even though the voices around her had turned silent as the man atop her ploughed her furrow relentlessly, she was conscious of a dozen unseen eyes watching, relishing her abuse. The man was slow and steady, dragging his prick across her hardened clit, driving the young woman to lust. She moaned piteously as she felt her loins burn with unwanted pleasure.

As her heat began to rise, Maddy stopped struggling. A fiery need for completion took control of her and she began to rock her hips to meet the onslaught of the steel hard shaft within her. Her breath became short and she began to utter little cries of passion at each stroke of the insistent prick. Just as she was building to her crescendo, the tape over her eyes was removed. In her passion, through the narrow apertures of her hood, she saw the face of her tormentor. His eyes were dark and his eyebrows bushy and black. A long, thick, black moustache adorned his mouth, which was smiling with delight. He grunted as his meat began to throb within her. Maddy's fevered tunnel began to contract and pulse as she felt the man's hot seed flood her womb. She cried out as she came, her enfeebled voice sounding more like a neigh, the tremors of her orgasm resounding throughout her body.

Maddy's sex was still pulsing with pleasure as the man drew his detumescing prick from within her. Through the fog of her post coital bliss, Maddy could hear the sounds of male approval all around. When the man stood up, her legs were released. She felt herself pulled to her feet. The man who had raped her patted her on the head and uttered some low, appreciative words. Through the slits of her hood, her tear filled eyes watched him as he mounted his horse and rode away.

CHAPTER TEN

Herman and Louise had been away for two and a half days. In the back of the van lay two young, nubile women. Twins. Herman had hit the jackpot. "Let Feeney try and lowball me on this one," he thought as he turned off of the Interstate onto Route 286 North. Twenty minutes and they would be safe at home, unloading their valuable cargo.

Louise's thoughts were on their charges locked deep under the ramshackle barn. She couldn't wait to get her cunt licked by the slut Maureen. She was so horny she almost asked Herman for a favor. She looked over at him, his fingers locked tight around the steering wheel, that stupid old tractor hat on his head. He would probably want her to suck his mangy old cock in return. The thought of it made her shudder. She could wait.

Jake and the boys had spent the last two days taking turns watching the monitors on Irving's laptop. The screen flipped between views every five seconds. Tucker, who was on watch, had gotten tired of watching the screen's incessant blinking from one scene to the next and had locked on to a single view which overlooked the entrance to the barn. He had been at it for two hours. He yawned. Leon was due up next. He got up to get a coke from the small room fridge. While his back was turned, a dark maroon van pulled onto the screen. After a few moments, a bulky, fiftyish, old lady got out and opened the barn door. The van slid inside and she followed it, closing the door behind her.

Tucker gave the screen a cursory glance when he came back with his coke. Satisfied that all was as it was, he sat down and took a long pull from the ice cold cola.

Herman laid the two new girls out on the floor next to the van. He hadn't been able to resist removing their matching, bright yellow, bikini tops when he and Louise had first grabbed them, but the narrow, licentious bottoms were still on. The girls both looked up wide eyed at their captors. Helping the seemingly helpless old lady had come second nature to them. She was effusive in her thanks as they lifted her heavy bags into the van. A jab from the Taser gun paralyzed them long enough for Herman to pull them in and tie them up. Goodbye, Panama City. Hello, life of degrading sexual abuse.

It didn't take long to get the unhappy, young females down into the hole. Herman snipped off their tiny, string-like bottoms with his penknife. Each girl sported a little yellow beard over her sex. Natural blonds. They both begged and pleaded when their temporary gags were removed. Louise quieted them quickly with the more permanent, thick, leather plugs. Once in their cages, she gave them a jolt from the electric wand just for good measure.

Maureen and the brown haired girl looked none too worse for wear. They drank gratefully from the water jugs once Louise got around to it. Herman stuck his cock in Maureen's cage. "Dessert first, slut," he told her, "then dinner."

Maureen's lips seized the flaccid meat with alacrity. Herman's eyes rolled back as he luxuriated in the fervent mouth. Maureen's skills had developed favorably over the weeks that she had been in captivity. Although she was anxious to earn her dinner, she knew that Herman would assess her blow job critically. She desperately wanted to eat.

While Herman got his rocks off, Louise washed down the brunette. "I'll decide when she eats," she thought to herself, her slit watering in anticipation of Maureen's worship at that shrine.

Herman was nearing fulfillment. He groaned deeply as he felt his stiff shaft fill with his seed. "Suck it, bitch!" he yelled. "Suck it!"

Maureen absorbed every drop of Herman's copious discharge. Three days on the road really built up a load.

"I'm going up," Herman told Louise as he tucked his now flaccid cock back into his pants.

Louise nodded. She had emptied a can of beans and franks out for the desperately hungry brunette. She then turned the hose on Maureen, washing away three days of sweat and grime. Motioning for her to turn around, she addressed her loins and ass, wiping them clean.

When she was finished, Maureen turned and stared at the old lady expectantly, her bound hands dangling from her collar. Louise finished washing away three days of wastes from the bottom of the cages. She opened a can of bean and franks and emptied it into a bowl on the floor. She opened Maureen's cage and motioned her to get out. "Come on out, my little cunt licker. Time for eating," she said.

Maureen eagerly exited the cage and began to crawl to the bowl.

"Not so fast, cunt!" Louise barked. "You've had desert, now the appetizer." The old lady sat down on a small stool and, spreading her legs, raised her dress to her waist. She pulled off her baggy cotton drawers. "Come and suck my twat, slut. Then you can feed your ugly face."

The poor girl grimaced. Her stomach ached with hunger. Although she had suffered almost every torture known to man as the prisoner of these two mad, cruel devils, she had not yet become fully inured to their degrading verbal abuse. "I'm not a slut," she thought to herself. "I'm not ugly." Her eyes glistening with tears, she lowered her head and crept between the callous woman's knees. Louise had placed the bowl of food on the floor directly beneath her quim. Maureen fought back the urge to bury her face in it. She had no desire to prompt a whipping.

As Maureen's lips and tongue addressed Louise's sweltering cunt, the old lady sighed with delight. "That's it, slut," she told the prostrate girl. "Nice and slow. Make it good or I'll whip your tits until they bleed!"

The two new girls looked on in disbelief. What kind of hell had they been brought to, they wondered fearfully. They looked at each other, tears in their eyes. Silenced by the rude, thick wands of leather in their mouths, separated by cold bars of steel, they could only comfort each with their forlorn eyes. Was this their future, they both asked themselves, praying that it would not be so.

Maureen's tongue delved deeply into Louise's sweaty puss. The old lady's musky discharge covered her face. Louise's hands were on the girl's head, gripping it tightly, as she felt her blood rising. When Maureen tickled her fat, stiff clit, Louise moaned. "Yessssssssss," she hissed. "That's the spot, slut. Keep licking it!" she ordered.

Louise's whole body contracted as her cunt throbbed and pulsed in orgasm. "Oh! Oh! Oh!" she yelled as the waves of pleasure shot through her. She closed her thighs around Maureen's head and pressed her mouth against her gash. "Oh! Oh! Oh!" she cried.

Mercifully, when her pussy's throbs petered out, Louise allowed Maureen to eat. The girl frantically sucked down the food. Louis laughed as she watched.

At the motel, Leon's eyes clouded over as he tried to maintain his attention on the actionless screen. He had missed it when Herman had left the barn and gone to the house. It was Jake who finally made note of the signs of activity. He looked over Leon's shoulder. He slapped Leon on the back of the head.

"Idiot!" he yelled. "The lights are on in the house!"

Leon jolted to attention. "What?" he said.

"The lights are on, idiot. Unlike your head, there's somebody home!"

"Oh," Leon replied sheepishly.

Irving and Leon played back the recording of the night's activity. They watched the van pull up to the barn and Louise get out and open the barn door.

"Well, if there wasn't anybody down in that cellar before," Irving challenged Jake, "there is now."

"Ok, ok," Jake replied. "But we're not making any move until someone shows up to collect them."

"That could be days," Irving replied.

"If it's days, it's days," Jake answered him. "We didn't put those girls, whoever they are, into that hole. If we weren't here, they'd be just where they are. They're not our responsibility."

Irving bristled. "So you say."

"Yes!" Jake relied emphatically. "So I say! Now you fix me up something that will let us know when someone pulls into that driveway, some kind of alarm. These dodo's can't keep awake watching a computer screen."

"I'll set up a motion detector," he offered.

"Good," Jake answered. "Just don't get caught. We've got to see whoever stops to pick up the merchandise."

Irving fought back the urge to challenge Jake's assessment of their responsibility to the kidnappers' victims.

The next morning Irving had the gear set up. Jake had instructed him to get a gizmo to track the pick up vehicle so they didn't have to follow it. The team spent three anxious days awaiting developments. They watched on the computer screen as Herman and Louise made their way back and forth to the barn. They were able to see as one or the other, or both, descended a ladder into the dungeon. Irving had added sound to the bug in the barn and they could hear occasional snatches of conversation as the two kidnappers walked from the barn door to the trapdoor and back.

On the third day, on Martinez's watch, Herman was seen bringing the girls up from the cellar one by one. The crew gathered around the computer screen as they watched three naked young women mounted in stocks. The camera had a powerful zoom lens and they were able to record the frightened faces of the women as they were trussed up for display.

Jake ordered Curley and Leon to go to the farm and get ready to plant the tracking device on whatever vehicle pulled in. About an hour later, the motion detector went off and a large delivery truck pulled up the driveway.

Chuckie was driving, and he backed the truck up to the barn door. Feeney stepped out of the passenger side and strolled to the barn. Chuckie followed. Jake and his crew watched as they entered the barn.

"Get a close up of their faces," Jake ordered. Irving remotely maneuvered the camera lens to record their identities. Leon was charged with getting a make on the truck and installing the 'gizmo'.

Irving panned the camera back as the two men entered the barn. They watched as Herman shook the thin one's hand. Herman and Louise stood by expectantly, awaiting Feeney's perusal of the product.

Irving and Jake watched with astonishment as the thin man pulled a gun from his jacket. There was a look of surprise followed instantly by alarm on the faces of the kidnappers. Two sharp, crisp shots rang out and the old man and lady fell to the floor. The thin man approached them and put two more shots in each one's head.

"Well, that party's over," Jake observed.

"Shit," was all Irving could say.

Feeney replaced the gun in his shoulder holster. Business was business. He had relayed his suspicions that Herman was getting ready to close shop to his overseas partners after the last trip. The fact that Herman had notified him of a new load so quickly reinforced his suspicions. Herman was not to be allowed to enjoy the benefit of his ill gotten gains. Loose lips sink ships.

The hooded and naked prisoners were quaking and moaning. One of them had peed. There was no mistaking the sound of gunshots in an enclosed environment like the barn. The sound of Herman and Louise dropping to the floor, uttering short, doleful moans, was confirmation of their demise, if any was necessary.

"Let's get to work," Feeney ordered Chuckie. Chuckie had been surprised at the summary execution of the old couple, but he shrugged his shoulders and got on with the business at hand. It took about an hour before all three girls were loaded on the truck. Leon had already wired the tracker and had recorded all of the vehicle's distinguishing characteristics.

Feeney had stood by, smoking, while Chuckie did his work. This was Chuckie's job and he was damned if he was going to do it for him. When Chuckie was done, Feeney nodded towards the two lifeless bodies. "Let's drop them down the hole," he said. "Then we gotta wash down this blood. I don't want these assholes found for a long time."

After unceremoniously tossing Louise and Herman's bodies down into the cellar, Chuckie got a hose from the house and washed the blood away. The water thinned out the deep red puddles until a reddish hue spread across the floor.

"In a couple of days you won't be able to tell the difference," Feeney said. He went over to close and lock the door to the dungeon.

"Hey," Chuckie said. "Is that fat broad down there?"

"How the hell do I know," Feeney answered him. "And what if she is?"

"Are we just going to leave her there?" Chuckie asked.

"I'm not going down there and neither are you. We're getting out of here, now."

Feeney's voice had the sharp edge of command.

Chuckie shrugged. "It just seems a waste," he said. "I mean a blow job is a blow job."

"You'll be giving my .22 a blow job in a minute if you don't get in the truck," Feeney responded.

After putting out the lights in the house and the barn and locking them both, the two men mounted the van. After a moment, it began to move forward and rocked gently as it navigated the ruts and potholes. It then disappeared from view.

Martinez and Tucker were waiting a few hundred yards down the road in the Taurus as the van pulled out. Jake called Martinez's cell phone.

"Is the beeper working?"

"Like a charm," Martinez answered.

"Stay a few hundred yards behind him at first, then drop back. If they pull off the road, don't worry. Irving's got a relay from the tracker here. We'll track them if they make any detours."

When Curley and Leon got back, Jake ordered everybody to pack up. Irving protested. "There's somebody down that cellar," he said. "You're not going to just leave her there, are you?"

"We don't have time to fuck around," Jake said.

Irving got up. "I don't care what you do, Jake. I'm going over there and I'm going into that basement. I'm getting whoever is in there out. If you want to stop me, you'll have to shoot me." He looked hotly into Jake's eyes. Jake had never seen him like this.

"Do you know what it's like to starve to death, Jake?" Irving asked him, his voice trembling.

"Okay, Okay," Jake relented. "But what do we do with her?"

"Call your big shot, Burnham," Irving replied. "Let him figure something out."

Curley and Leon finished packing up the stuff as Jake and Irving drove down to the farm. Jake made them stop a hundred yards from the driveway.

"Why're we stopping?" Irving asked.

"I'm not adding my tire tracks to the evidence log once those two dirtbags are found," Jake answered. "We're getting out here and walking in. We'll walk the girl out. Since we're here, you might as well be of some use. I'll go down to the cellar of the barn, you get on the computer and transfer the money to this account." He handed Irving a piece of paper with an offshore bank's name on it and a long string of numbers. "This is between me and you. Got it?"

Irving smiled. "Got it."

Jake unlocked the barn with no problem. The lock on the trapdoor was a little more difficult. But he had picked tougher locks and after a few moments, the bolt slid open.

Maureen had watched as Herman and Louise's bodies had come crashing down into the underground prison. She could tell right away that they were dead. She froze in terror when she heard the trapdoor slam closed and the bolt shot home. She was gagged and bound, captive in her little steel cage. Her body crumpled in despair. She knew now that she was going to die a long and excruciating death.

Her heart leapt when she heard the trap door open again. But as she watched the legs descend, she realized that whoever it was might be coming down to finish her off. When Jake reached the bottom of the ladder and turned to see her, his cold, hard visage brought her no comfort.

Jake took in the sight of the miserable girl. "Irving was right," he thought. When he approached the cage, the frightened girl drew her body back as far as it would go.

"I'm not going to hurt you," he told her. "I'm getting you out of here. Where's the key to the cage?"

Maureen began to cry with relief. She nodded her head towards a hook on the wall. Jake took the key and unlocked the cage. Hesitatingly, the naked, heavyset girl crawled out. Jake carefully drew her to her feet. Maureen's eyes were flooded with tears.

"I'm going to unlock your hands and remove your gag. You have to be absolutely quiet. Do you understand?"

Maureen nodded energetically.

He removed the chain and collar from the naked girl and unbuckled the gag from behind her head.

"Oh, thank you, mister, thank you," Maureen blubbered.

"Shhhhhhh!" Jake remonstrated. "You have to be quiet. Can you make it up the ladder?"

Maureen nodded. "I think so," she said, her body quivering.

When Jake got the naked girl up the ladder, he relocked the trapdoor and carefully replaced the pallets on top of it. He took Maureen's hand and led her to the house. When they entered, Irving had just completed the transfer of the money.

"Take her upstairs and give her a shower," he instructed Irving. "Don't let her out of your sight. Give her some of the old lady's clothes and feed her. I'm going to call Burnham."

Burnham answered his cell phone on the second ring. Jake brought him up to date. Then he told him about the girl.

"What the fuck am I supposed to do with her?" Burnham screamed into the phone.

"Listen," Jake told him. "Either you make some arrangements pronto to get this girl somewhere where she can be treated and held incommunicado or this job's over right now."

There was silence on the phone. After a few moments, Burnham responded. "All right. I can probably get a long distance ambulance there in a couple of hours. I'll find someplace to stash her. But if this fucks up the deal on Maddy, you're a dead man, Jake."

"Many people have tried," Jake answered.

* * * * * * * * * * *

Maddy was rendered numb by her assault. Docilely, she watched the tall, dark eyed man who had raped her ride away. She had the feeling that some line had been crossed and that her almost ceremonial ravishment marked the beginning of her new life. Her wrists strained at the buckles that held them high behind her back. She discovered that she was crying. A feeling of dark foreboding came over her as she watched the man recede into the distance through her hood's narrow apertures.

The despondent girl was able to see only small swatches of the landscape around her. There were long lines of white rail fences around what looked like a dirt track. A large house stood in the distance.   There were several outbuildings. To her astonishment, she thought she saw a tall, hooded, naked woman pulling a cart.

That was exactly what Maddy had seen. Standing next to the young girl, watching over his new charge, was Maddy's trainer, Anton Drabik. Drabik was a former colonel in the Red Army. Times had been tough when the former Soviet Union collapsed and it was many months following his discharge 'for economic reasons' that he had been able to get any kind of a decent job. His skill as a killer of men, well honed in the Afghanistan fiasco, was the only skill had had to market. It didn't take long for him to be recruited by one of the new 'mafias' that had sprung up. He had risen quickly in the organization and now worked as an assassin and part time trainer of ponygirls for Axmail Grobgy, himself a former KGB apparatchik.

It was Grobgy who had sampled Maddy's cunt just now. He was her new owner and master. He also commanded a virtually tribal clan of steel eyed, ruthless gangsters who controlled 35% of the heroin smuggled into the new Russian and Ukrainian Republics. His 'family' had extorted themselves into significant shares of hundreds of legitimate businesses. There was a special market they ran outside of Odessa specializing in 'hard to find' items such as weapons, identification papers, car parts, and, some alleged fissionable material.

Untold wealth had fallen into the coffers of a fortunate few since the fall of the 'Evil Empire'. The three dozen or so newly minted multi-millionaires that had taken up residence in central Kalikastan had purchased huge estates, most of them former communal farms, and resumed the sports and hobbies of their capitalistic and feudal forbears. Among the ancient traditions of the raiders of the

Kalikastan steppes was the sport of pony racing. Female, human ponies, that is.

The rules of the sport were simple. All women recruited to serve as human thoroughbreds were to be of non-Slavic origin. This prevented the sportsmen from drawing on hundreds of thousands of nubile women in many of the former Soviet Republics who might otherwise grace their paddocks. Females from countries that were the traditional enemies of the Workers' Paradise were especially prized. Americans, Britons, Germans, Poles, and other Western European females were numbered among the prime pony flesh. Drawing on centuries old enmities, Swedes and Hungarians were treasured. Maddy was potentially, given her large but graceful physique and her American origins, a natural for the sport.

The six foot four inch tall Drabik was the ace of Grobgy's trainers. He knew good pony flesh when he saw it and this new girl had great potential. All would depend on her training. All thoughts of her humanity must be driven from her. She must learn that she is merely a chattel, albeit a valuable one, existing only to please the lusts and desires of her master and his guests and servants.

Maddy's opportunity to take in her new surroundings was cut short by a pull on her leash. Fearfully she followed the lead. She could see the broad back of a man walking purposely before her. He was wearing a dark blue tee shirt and jeans. His hair was long and black, descending loosely to his shoulders.

They were walking quickly along a dirt pathway. Maddy struggled to keep up, fearing the consequences if she should stumble and fall. She saw that they were approaching a huge, white, barn-like building. On the peak of the building was a large crest, consisting of a yellow, rampant wolf on a field of blue, its talons raised to strike.

Underneath the fiercely depicted wolf was an inscribed motto, "Sub Hoc Signo Vinces" - Under this sign we shall conquer.

When they reached the building, the man slid open a large wooden door set on a track. The inside of the barn was dimly lit and Maddy had trouble making out any details. Before her eyes could adjust fully, she felt herself pulled further into the barn.

They stopped in the middle of an open area. Maddy could see what looked like a warren of wooden stalls on either side. There were large wooden beams above her. A chain dangled from one of them.

Drabik stood back and made a visual inspection of the naked girl. He admired the well toned, muscled flanks, the broad chest, the taut belly. He ran his hand over the leather hood covering Maddy's shaved head and stroked the long, reddish brown hair that jutted from the hood's rear. Maddy tried to pull away when he reached out for her breasts, but was brought back by a sudden and rough jerk on her leash. The man frightened Maddy. His face was clean shaven, but he had large bushy eyebrows and a hard, piercing gaze.

As Drabik caressed her breasts, Maddy could feel the strength of his well calloused hands. He pulled at her nipples, pinching them hard, and drew a small yelp of protest from the girl. He then took her by the shoulders and turned her around. He ran his hands down her thighs, assessing them, pleased by what he found.

Maddy was overwhelmed by the freedom with which the man handled her body. It was as if it was no longer hers, or rather, that it belonged to him. She felt her wrists behind her back being unfastened from the leather harness she had worn now for almost 24 hours. She uttered a sigh of relief as she was allowed to lower them. She felt the harness being unbuckled and removed from her body.

The barn was oddly quiet. Maddy heard the harness fall to the dark wooden floor as it was tossed aside by the man. She heard the sound of the chain that hung from the joist above her being pulled down. The man clipped it to the leather bracelet on her right wrist and then quickly spun her around. By the time Maddy realized what was happening, the left wrist had been affixed to the chain and the man was pulling on the opposite end. Her arms were quickly forced to rise over her head. The man pulled on the chain until Maddy was standing on the tips of her toes. He stepped over to a large wooden vertical beam and fastened it to a hook embedded there about seven feet above the floor.

There was little doubt in Maddy's mind as to what was going to happen next. She remembered well the whipping of the red headed girl the day of her arrival. She began to whine and moan. She tried to beg the man through her still gagged mouth to spare her. The result was a strangely garbled, piteous sound.

Drabik stepped up to Maddy and ran his rough hands over her skin. He massaged her breasts, grabbing them firmly, circling them with his long, steel hard fingers. She grimaced as he squeezed them in a vice-like grip. He pressed his hand between her thighs and caught her labial lips between his thumb and forefinger, pinching them cruelly. Maddy moaned in pain.

Seemingly satisfied that he had Maddy's full attention, he walked over to a rack of whips that hung along the outer wall of one of the stalls. He selected a long, thin, leather encased reed. Maddy tried to plead again frantically as she watched him test its strength and swish it through the air. He stepped behind her, his thick soled boots making a heavy, thudding sound on the hard wooden floor. He circled her twice, swishing the reed back and forth, eying her lustfully. Maddy tried to keep up with him, spinning on her toes so that she could keep him in view, a difficult task given the narrow slits in her leather hood.

He had gone out of view behind her when he struck the first blow. There was a hissing sound and then a loud, 'crack!' as the whip struck across her back. Maddy howled with pain. The kiss of the reed drew a line of fire across her tender skin.

Drabik maintained his steady pace around the moaning and pleading girl. 'Crack!' A blow landed across the front of her thighs. 'Crack!' The reed lacerated the flesh of her buttocks. 'Crack!' Maddy felt the whip's bite across her breasts.

For ten minutes, Drabik kept circling the unfortunate girl, striking out seemingly at random. He struck every part of the poor girl's body that he could reach. Each blow left a red line of abused skin in its wake. Maddy's throat was growing hoarse from her screaming. Tears flowed from her eyes, creating streams down the tight hood that dominated her face. She could feel them drip onto her chest as she awaited the cruel man's next blow. She had given up trying to follow his gyrations around her and stood still, taking whatever the man decided to give her.

When he was finished, Maddy hung limply from the chain. Her chest heaved with her sobs. Her voice was a long, wailing moan. She heard the man's footsteps as he went to the beam and unhooked the chain. He slowly lowered it until Maddy was on her knees and then he tied it off again. Maddy looked up at him through the narrow slits in her hood. Her eyes were befogged with tears. He stepped up to her and unbuckled the gag from behind her head. Maddy began to beg and plead. "Please don't whip me any more, please...."

Her entreaties were interrupted by a mighty slap across her face. The force of the hand stunned the forlorn girl. Twice more, the man lashed out at her with his hands, alternating with his right and left. Even though her face was covered by the leather hood, the blows stung fiercely and Maddy saw stars as her jaw was rocked back and forth.

Still sobbing woefully, Maddy held her tongue. The man's message was clear: no talking. He waited until she was recovered and then he lowered the zipper to his pants. He fished out a long, fat cock already hardening with lust. The young girl cringed as she realized that she was about to be assaulted again. Her stomach turned at the prospect of her imminent oral ravishment.

Drabik grabbed Maddy's long pony tail with one fist and pinched open her jaw with the other. She felt the thick meat pass over her lips and into her mouth. Maddy desired desperately, above all else, to avoid displeasing this callous and cruel man. She accepted the rigid pole and worked her lips and tongue around it. The man began to fuck her mouth and she strained to pleasure it each time he drove it remorselessly past her fervent lips. Again and again, the man pressed his cock home, striking the back of Maddy's mouth, piercing the entrance to her throat. Maddy looked up through the tiny slits in her hood and saw the cruel man peering down at her. He held her eyes, mesmerizing her, as he drew his cock over her pursed lips. She heard him groan and her mouth was flooded with his hot, creamy discharge. He pushed his cock deeper into her, jetting his come inside her throat. He groaned again. His fist firmly clutched the stream of hair that flowed from the back of her head. Maddy gagged as the throbbing rod filled her esophagus.

Gratefully, the unhappy girl felt the pulsing of his cock begin to ease. He withdrew from her mouth slowly and deliberately, making sure that every drop of his come was deposited inside. When he finally exited, he rubbed its still semi-hard and slimy head over Maddy's lips and chin, capping her degradation.

Maddy received Drabik's insult stoically. It was clear to her that she was trapped in some low level of hell and that there was nothing she could do about it. No one she knew or knew her had any conception of where she was. Even she didn't know. All she had seen since her delivery to this strange, cruel country was the courtyard of the cruel way station for enslaved women she had been in yesterday, and the brief glimpse she had had today of her new surroundings, viewed through the tiny slits of her hood.

The potential costs of protest or resistance had been made very clear, however. Whatever fate had in store for her, wherever this strange nightmare led, she would have to endure it if she wanted to live. And for now, she desperately did.

Having initiated the new slave into the rigors of her servitude, Drabik put his flaccid tool away. There was more work to do.

Drabik disappeared from Maddy's sight for a few moments. She remained kneeling, her hands suspended over her head. She could see in the dim light the varied whips and other instruments of correction displayed on the wall before her. Her stomach grew queasy as she sensed that she would become better acquainted with them before too long. Her heart ached, ready to break, when she thought of the pain and suffering she would have to endure. She vowed to do all she could to avoid it. She would obey, enthusiastically, every order issued to her, would suffer any indignity rather than provoke another beating.

Maddy heard Drabik approach her from behind and felt his hands circle her throat unlocking the thick, leather collar that she had been adorned with the previous day. Maddy dared not turn and look to observe what the Drabik was up to behind her. Ominously, she felt a tape measure stretched around her neck. Drabik took careful measurements and, when he was done, stepped away.

She heard his boots retreat and then return. She felt a hard, leather encased, plastic collar, thicker and larger than the other, placed round her neck. While the prior collar had prevented her from lowering her head, this one, much higher in front than in the back, pressed on her chin, raising her whole head upwards. It was black and bore the Grobgy crest emblazoned on a metal disk fastened at its center. Steel rings bedecked its sides, back and front. A long, wide, thick strap ran down the middle of her back.

Maddy instinctively tried to straighten her back and raise herself up on her knees to compensate for the forced uplift of her face. The stiff, uncomfortable collar was a harbinger to Maddy of more cruel accouterments to come. She whined, unintentionally, and a tear ran down her cheek. She flexed and writhed her bound hands above her in frustration and fear. If she did not still suffer the reality of the burning strokes of the whip, she could believe that she was in some horrible nightmare. She thought, with misery, of home, of her apartment, of her family. They all seemed to belong to a world that had ceased to exist.

Next to be applied to Maddy's body was what she would come to learn was her training hood. It was made from a soft, blue, stretchy material rather than leather. The resilience of the fabric allowed it to be stretched so that it fit tightly against the head and face, homogenizing the wearer's features. It could be left on for lengthy periods since its design was to allow the skin beneath it to breathe. She felt her leather hood being pulled up and removed. A wave of relief swept through her now that her full sight had been restored. She had resumed human status. She had a face! She was a person!

Drabik was careful, as he stood behind the female, to keep her now naked face pointed away from him. He had no desire to see it. To him, she was no longer a human being and her facial appearance was of no moment. She would remain, as long as she was a ponygirl, and that would be forever, a faceless creature whose identity was known to none.

Maddy felt the hood being slid up her long, auburn pony tail and then stretched to fit over her head. Once she realized that she was being rehooded, forgetting her resolution to endure passively the whims of her masters, she began to bob and weave her head desperately, attempting to avoid restoration of the depersonalization of her face and the curtailment of her sight. Drabik was not unprepared for resistance.

He placed his hands on Maddy's shoulders and squeezed its pressure points in an iron grip. Maddy screamed in pain. He held the points for thirty seconds, allowing Maddy to languish at the mercy of his brutal hands. When he finally relented, Maddy, properly chastised, forlornly permitted the hood to be applied.

The soft, thick hood clung tightly to her face, accentuating its contours. It fit, literally, like a glove. The openings for her eyes were like tiny dots, narrowing her vision to a small circle. The hood had a wide, oval opening for her mouth and two small holes for her nostrils. It descended over her chin and down to the top edge of her collar. Small hooks in the bottom of the hood attached to little eyelets in the collar, allowing the hood to be pulled taut.

Maddy was now covered from the bottom of her neck to the top of her head. Drabik released her wrists from the chain above her one by one, replacing her thick, brown, leather bracelets with ones of black. The bracelets were then attached to clips in the long strap that descended down her back.

When Drabik finished affixing Maddy's wrists behind her, he placed a thick leather encased bit into her mouth. It had a steel plate that depressed her tongue, and straps on the sides that permitted it to be connected to the sides of the hood. Drabik tested the effectiveness of the bit by pulling on the rings to which it was attached. Maddy felt the steel plate press down harshly on her tongue. The pain was excruciating. She moaned and cried, and tried to assuage the pain by moving her head backwards. But Drabik had his hands firmly on her head and held it steady as he maintained the tautness on the straps. When he was satisfied that she had learned the purpose of the steel plate on her tongue, he relented.

Maddy whined in self pity. The lesson of the functionality of the bit, when melded with the surreal apparition she had seen earlier of a woman pulling a cart, gave rise to a horrible thought. Horses wore bits in their mouths; horses pulled carts. Was she being made into some kind of a human horse? Was such a thing possible? Her mind reeled at the thought.

Maddy had no more time to speculate on her new status, for Drabik pulled her to her feet by her hair. She cried out in pain as he pulled her to a short wooden bench and shoved her down upon it. He removed the boots that her been installed on her feet the day before. She sat and watched as Drabik measured her naked feet. He left and returned with two long, black boots. He straddled her body, his back to her, and pulled them onto her feet. They had hard bottoms, with a built in arch support. The tops were of supple leather and fastened to her upper shins by a belt.

There was a ring in the center of Maddy's collar and Drabik used it to drag the outfitted girl to her feet. He attached a long leather lead to it and pulled her to the door of the barn. There was a full length mirror there that Maddy had failed to notice when she had been brought inside. Drabik presented her to it. He held her still, his hand gripping the ring in the front of her collar. He bent her head down slightly so that she could get a good look at herself. Maddy sobbed in dismay as she viewed a faceless, naked beast before her. She moaned and her knees sagged as she was overcome with despair. What had this man made of her? Was she really the same person as the apparition she viewed before her?

Drabik broke the spell that the sight of her own dehumanized body had cast over her by opening the sliding door and pulling her through. She was blinded by the bright sunlight. The narrow openings in her hood seemed to make the sun's glare worse. She felt herself pulled forwards and she scrambled to keep up with her tormentor.

It was Drabik's practice to put the new ponygirls to work as soon as possible. He led the unfortunate girl to a sandy ring with a tall post in the middle. A long pole extended from the post. A chain hung from its end. Drabik affixed a small chain with a ring in the middle to the sides of the bit. He attached the chain from the pole to the ring, drawing it taut. He took up a long, thin, switch, with a slim leather thong attached. Stepping over to a small electric motor at the center of the post, he turned it on. He snapped the switch at the girl's buttocks. It landed with a loud, 'crack' and Maddy jumped forwards. Maddy felt a tug on the bit in her mouth as the pole above her began to pull her ahead. Three more slaps with the whip and Maddy moved hurriedly to maintain its pace.

For well over twenty minutes, Maddy circled the post, placing one foot ahead of the other, plodding at a dull, leisurely trot. She could see little through the little holes in her hood except what was directly before her. The tight pull of the pole on her bit kept her head from moving from side to side. She sensed, rather than saw, her trainer watching her intently. Her naked breasts bounced and swung up and down and side to side with each loping stride. She wanted to beg the man to let her stop, to free her. She wanted this horrible nightmare to end. But the pole dragged her relentlessly along the circular path.

Suddenly, Maddy heard the wine of the electric motor increase in tempo and the pole began to pull harder at her bit. She increased her pace to keep up. Her breath began to become ragged as her chest heaved to draw in enough oxygen to feed her bloodstream. She was marching along now at double time, the dull throbbing in her thighs and hips becoming exquisitely painful. The fact that her hands were bound behind her caused her shoulders to ache with every swing of her torso and made it exceedingly difficult to maintain her balance as she was herded along. Maddy tried to call out for mercy, but all that emerged was a gargled groan.

As the ponygirl circled the ring at her quickened pace, her lord and master rode up. He was accompanied by a languidly beautiful young woman, barely out of her teens, with long black hair and pale white skin. She was wearing a white blouse and black, leather jodhpurs, tall, black leather boots. She sat on a large, sturdy white horse, wet with sweat. Maddy saw the dim outline of the couple as they dismounted their horses. The next time around the ring she saw that they had approached the circle of sand and were watching her struggle desperately to maintain the pace set by the remorseless pole.

Grobgy was accompanied by his daughter, Anya. She was his pride and joy and had been raised to relish the cruel and merciless exercise of power. She had no delusions as to the nature of her father's business and the source of their now staggering wealth. She liked to watch the ponygirls put through their paces. Her father had been telling her about the new female and she had been anxious to see her.

"A beautiful specimen, Father. Look how her tits fly as she runs."

Grobgy laughed. "And she's a hot young filly, too. She couldn't get enough of my cock earlier this morning."

Anya slapped her father's shoulder playfully. "Respect me, Father. I'm a delicate flower. I don't need to know about your rutting with the ponygirls."

"And what about you?" Grobgy replied. "I've heard that you've removed their bits for some fun from time to time."

It was Anya's turn to laugh. "Oh, Father, you're making me blush."

"If only I could, Anya. If only I could."

The lord and lady of the manor watched with interest as Drabik increased the pace of the pole yet again. He nodded at the pair.

Maddy felt the pole increase its relentless pull on her bit. She was running now, her legs screaming with pain, her chest straining for air. Three times around the post she sprinted to keep up, franticly fearful of the consequences of failure. She knew that she would soon collapse with exhaustion; it was just a matter of time. On the fourth circuit, her right leg caught the back of her left and she stumbled. The sturdy pole dragged her behind it.

Drabik quickly halted the pole's movement lest it break the pony's neck. He grabbed the switch and lashed out at her three times. Maddy, in panic, tried to struggle to her feet, but she was overcome with exhaustion and had not the strength to do so. She cried out as each kiss of the switch burned into her buttocks.

Grobgy and his daughter laughed with amusement at Maddy's predicament. They knew that Drabik would have this female sprinting with the best of them in no time. For now, her futile struggle to find her feet and avoid the lash were comical to them.

Drabik grabbed Maddy's hair and pulled her to her feet. She groaned with pain at the seizure of her hair. When back on her feet, Drabik released the bit from the pole and pulled her towards her admirers.

Maddy was huffing and puffing from her tormenting exercise. Her generous breasts rose and fell, jiggling delightfully with each frantic breath. Maddy saw the couple staring at her. She recognized Grobgy as her rapist from that morning and was appalled at the frank appraisal of her naked form by the attractive, refined, young woman who was standing next to him. She pulled her legs together unconsciously, humiliated at the exposure of her lightly shrouded sex.

Drabik noted Maddy's reaction and, after grabbing her pony tail and pulling her head back, slapped her across the breasts twice. Maddy cringed at the stinging blows. He grabbed her right thigh and pulled on it, spreading her legs apart. This is how ponygirls stand before their betters.

"Good work, Anton," Anya complemented him in Russian. "You've got her started off right."

"I've just gotten her started you mean," Drabik replied. "She's got a lot of potential, but she has to be taught her status right away." Drabik grabbed one of the breasts he had just slapped around and squeezed it gently, cupping it in his hand.

"Make her dance for us, Drabik," Anya challenged. "Let's see how hot she really is."

Maddy could not decipher the meaning of the Slavic words being bandied between the couple and her trainer. She knew that what they said involved her and whatever nefarious plans they had in store for her. She was taken aback when Drabik seized one of her still stinging breasts and began to caress it gently. His large hand cupped the sweaty, pale globe. She grew uncomfortable when she felt him tease her nipple with his thumb. She felt it stiffen and quickly looked at the woman to see if she had observed it. The woman was looking at her intently and seemed to smile as Drabik pulled gently on the nipple, extending it, pinching it softly.

Drabik stood behind Maddy and seized both her breasts with his hands while pressing his body up against her back. His hands massaged her sensitive globes, causing a tingling in her loins. The girl squirmed in frustration, mortified that her reactions to these unwanted caresses should be viewed by this beautiful, regal woman.

The rubbing of her breasts caused Maddy to moan. As a wave of pleasure ran through her, she allowed her body to relax, swimming in the comforting sensations. When she felt the hands of her possessor slink down her belly to the apex of her thighs, she shook herself awake. She knew the tantalizing hands' ultimate goal and her sense of humiliation and shame was renewed. "Not here!" she thought. "Not here in front of these people!"

Drabik's hands danced over her thighs and belly. As the mortified girl tried to squirm away, he circled her body under her breasts with one arm, holding her close to him. The other hand snaked its way to her loins, rubbing her belly and then descended to her snatch.

The trainer's hand found Maddy's sex moist and engorged. She whimpered when she felt him probe her burning tunnel with his fingers. She yearned to close her legs, to deny this beast that used her so callously access to her hot labial lips, but feared to disobey the command implicit in his separating them a few moments before.

Anya looked on appreciatively. "She's hot all right," she said to her father.

Grobgy did not reply, concentrated as he was on the compelling beauty of the impassioned, young female.

Maddy could feel her juices rising. Her pussy yearned for the man's practiced touch. She moaned as he began to torment the little bud of pleasure at the tip of her sheath. Now, oblivious to those who were watching her, she began to rub her loins against the hand that violated her, seeking its penetration of her lusting hole.

Drabik, sensing the increasing passion of his prisoner, thrust his fingers inside her, spreading her moistness to her clit, alternating between stroking the hot interior of her flush canal and rubbing the nub of pleasure above it. Maddy began to thrust her hips in time with the exploration of her sex. Her breath became short as she felt her need to complete this act of passion rising within her. As her orgasm flooded through her, her pussy throbbed and contracted around the fingers that tormented her. She rolled her head back and sagged at her knees as her body was awash with exquisite sensation. Drabik held her up, refusing to relent when her first wave of passion had passed. As Maddy felt the tingling of her loins renew, she became aware that the man intended to make her come again. She whined, desperately ashamed at the lustful display she was making of herself. She could not resist the incessant, demanding hand, and it was not long before she erupted again in orgasm, her whole body shaking and trembling, her breasts aching as they tightened, filled with her hot blood. She called out unwillingly, the sounds of her voice almost inhuman as she cried out, "Oh! Oh! Oh!"

Maddy was limp in her trainer's arms as the leavings of her orgasm flowed through her. She tried to regain her feet, but her legs were wobbly and she needed Drabik's strong grasp to steady her.

Anya was pleased and amused at the show. She clapped her hands enthusiastically. "Bravo, Anton! A wonderful performance!" she said, laughing.

"I told you," her father said to her.

"Well," Anya replied, "almost any woman would melt in Drabik's arms, Father. He seems unusually experienced in handling a cunt."

Anya knew of Drabik's skills with a cunt personally. They dallied together from time to time at an inn not too far from her father's estate. She felt a tinge of jealousy as she watched the ponygirl struggle to recover from her ordeal. Her own loins burned for his touch. "Maybe tonight," she thought.

Drabik knew better than to display any familiarity with his boss's daughter. She was his prize and he had shot men before for becoming too friendly with her. Oh, he permitted her little dalliances with the ponygirls, that was understandable. But her virtue with men he protected like a miser protecting his hoard. So far no man had proved worthy of her in his mind.

Anya's thoughts echoed in Drabik's mind. But Drabik had work to do. And work must come first. "May I proceed, Axmailavich?" he asked his boss.

"Da," Grobgy answered. "Come, Anya, lets to the house and have lunch"

Anya nodded, all the time watching Drabik's eyes. "He will be fucking the ponygirl tonight," she thought. "Not me." She turned and mounted her horse. With a flick of her riding whip, the horse jumped and dashed away, her father and his horse right behind her.

CHAPTER ELEVEN

It was the late afternoon when an exhausted Maddy was led back to the barn. Her maddeningly relentless and monotonous tour of the sandy pit had continued all day. Each time she would be started out slowly, only to have the pace increased until she was being led at a dead run. She would have been less despondent, and her backside less sore, if her abilities had progressed during the afternoon. But the constant movement had tired her, and by the end of the day she was tripping all over herself.

Between each session, she was allowed to rest and, at midday, she was given porridge to eat. Drabik removed her bit and squeezed the mixture of vitamins, milk and high protein, whole grain cereal into her mouth from a plastic bag. She consumed the bland mixture greedily. She was kept well watered and Drabik was careful not to exceed her pitiable abilities.

During the course of the day, Maddy saw a number of other ponygirls being led to and fro. She caught only glimpses of them as she whirled around her post, but it was enough to frighten her. They were dressed like she was, their features obscured by their hoods. Rough looking men and sallow youths led them by leashes that led to the ring in the front of their collar or to the thick, gold rings in their noses, a feature that Maddy had yet to acquire. Maddy saw a team of two women pulling a lightweight cart, with a skinny youth driving it. She heard the crack of a whip and the next time she saw the women, they were hurriedly propelling the cart off into the distance.

When Maddy entered the barn, it was a hive of activity. Naked, hooded women were being led to and from their stalls. Maddy brushed up against one and she got a fleeting glimpse of a pair of forlorn eyes through the tiny holes in the hood.

She had only a few moments to study the other ponygirls. She was quickly led by Drabik through a maze like corridor to one of the stalls. Unlike the stalls at the way station, these stalls had wooden swinging doors that reached down to two feet above the floor and blocked the view from inside and out. The stalls were ten by fifteen feet, longer than they were wide. Their walls were about eight feet high and did not rise all the way to the ceiling. As a result, the noises of the busy barn were readily discernable from inside. In one of the corners nearest the door, there was a shower hose attachment and a drain. A small closet sat along the opposite wall. At the rear of the stall was a long padded rail about 4' from the wall. Rings were mounted at various strategic places.

Once inside, Maddy's leash was released. Drabik removed the bit, and the collar, leaving her dehumanizing hood in place. He released her wrists and removed the bracelets. He took off her boots. But for her hood, Maddy was completely naked. He turned her body towards the wall and, after seizing both sides of her head to emphasize the need to keep it still, removed its covering. He took her hands and placed them in the air, over her head. She held them there, nervous as to the man's purpose. But she soon learned that is was benign enough as he began to stream a flow of cold water over her aching body.

It was strange to feel the flow of water over her bald scalp. It reminded her of what must be her grotesque appearance. She pushed this thought aside as she enjoyed the refreshing sheen of water that flowed down her torso and to her sore legs. When she was fully drenched, Drabik, standing behind her, took a soapy sponge and rubbed her body with it. Up and down her legs, over her buttocks, under her arms. When her whole body had been soaped, including her face and naked head, Drabik rinsed her off. He dried her with a soft towel and applied a soothing cream to her neck, face and scalp.

Drabik then released the fastenings holding Maddy's ponytail together. Her hair flowed freely for the first time since she left the way station. It was strange to Maddy to feel it loose on her naked back.   The man ran water through the long, thick cascade of hair that sprung from the rear of her head and shampooed it. There was an electric hair dryer, and Drabik dried the hair and combed it out. When done, he joined it together again, using the fastenings he had removed before.

Maddy felt that the man's efforts were caring, almost tender. Although he had hurt her, humiliated her, used her mouth with his thick, hard cock, he was meticulous with the care of her body. She realized that he needed to take care of her. She was valuable property. She had been acquired from thousands of miles away to serve here as a ponygirl and needs be that she be kept healthy and clean.

She was brought back to reality when Drabik restored the uncomfortable collar and reclipped her wrists behind her back. She grimaced with dismay as she watched him from the corner of her eye pull a new, clean, stretchy hood from the closet. She did not struggle this time as he placed it over her docile head and restored the steel bit to her mouth. Maddy again was a person no more.

Drabik took a specially designed board and placed it on the railing that ran the width of the room. It locked into a groove on the rail and there was just enough room left to mount Maddy's ass on it. He then pushed the board back, fixing its top in place against the rear wall of the stall. He lifted Maddy so that her rear end rested on the rail and then leaned her back on the board and belted her neck and torso in place. Drabik then grabbed an ankle and buckled the end of a thick, leather belt around it. He raised the ankle almost level with her torso, bending her knee, and affixed the other end of the strap to the rail. When he had done the other ankle, Maddy was leaning back, her eyes fixed on the ceiling above through the small holes in her hood, and her knees and ankles spread wide apart like the wings of a butterfly, raising her bottom slightly.

Maddy's spread legs revealed her sex and its hairy, reddish brown thatch. Her knees were bent and her widespread ankles were affixed to the rail within inches of her thighs. Knowing that everything that this cruel man did to her had its own purpose, Maddy struggled to see him, to learn his intent, but the angle of her collar prevented her from lowering her head enough to bring the man within her hood's narrowly focused apertures.

She could hear the man scraping something in what sounded like a metal bowl. She recalled the sound that had been made just before her head was shaved. Maddy realized then that she was about to have her pubic hair removed. She balked at this further measure of control over her body, squirming in her bonds, struggling futilely to bring her legs together. She made garbled sounds of protest from her grotesquely spread open mouth. One more mark of her individuality was going to be taken from her. Her sex would henceforth be bare, virtually indistinguishable from any other. Maddy had grown up a modest girl and had rarely worn revealing clothes as a teenager or as a young adult. All day, the thought of her nakedness before all the world had haunted and shamed her. Now she would be even more naked. All privacy, all personality was being stripped away.

Drabik was mixing some soap with water in a small steel bowl. He lathered it up with a brush. When Drabik began to apply the foamy soap onto her bush, Maddy tried to rock her hips to frustrate his mission. The hard man had a simple solution to her attempt to frustrate his will. He grabbed Maddy's clit between his thumb and forefinger and squeezed hard. Maddy moaned in anguish. The pain spread throughout her loins like a virus. Drabik waited until the girl was near to tears before releasing his tiny prisoner. Now she would cooperate.

Maddy cried as Drabik carefully removed swath after swath of hair. She knew that her naked loins would now invite use, as her tender nether lips and the slit that they guarded would be clearly displayed. She recalled the shame and repugnance she felt when her owner that morning had filled her womb with his conscienceless prick, and when, later, her trainer had manipulated her to unwanted pleasure. So much of what was happening to her involved the callous use of her body. How many men would she be forced to fuck? How many men would press their hardened manhoods into her mouth?

Each scrape of the razor brought a new cascade of tears to Maddy's eyes. She could feel the sharp razor drag across her pudenda. Where it passed, she felt her cool and wet, naked skin.

Ultimately, Maddy resigned herself to the loss of her pubic growth. As she let her mind drift, wondering what other indignities she would be forced to endure, she remembered the golden rings she had seen in the noses of the other women. She knew that it was only a matter of time before she acquired hers. She feared the pain of having her septum pierced, the humiliation she knew that she would experience at being ringed like an animal, guided by her nose from place to place. She closed her eyes in despair.

When Maddy's cunt was nice and clean shaven, Drabik wiped off the remaining soap with a wet cloth. He admired the pretty little thing, running his hand over the smooth surface. He tickled the nubbin of pleasure at the apex of the girl's cunt, worrying it into hardness, until Maddy's hips began to rock subtly and he saw a tell tale gleam appear between the engorging lips.

The ponygirl was mounted at just the right height for penetration. Drabik pulled his hardening tool from its lair and pressed it against the softening lips of Maddy's pussy. He teased the cunt entrance with his cock, rubbing it against the length of the moistening gash, pressing it against the girl's tingling clit. He waited until she moaned with enforced lust before he pressed his meat home.

Maddy moaned with frustration and revulsion as she felt her sheath filled with her trainer's cock. It was as if he had read her mind and wanted to confirm her worst fears. The girl desperately wanted to expel the hot, hard intruder. She cried out a garbled protest from behind the leather bit and shook and strained at her bonds. Drabik smiled as he saw her futile struggle. Maddy's pussy was tight and hot, and he sighed as he drew his cock deliberately back and forth inside her. As Drabik slowly ploughed her moist, hot slit, Maddy began to feel her need for satisfaction rise. She felt the rough hands of the man run along the soft interior of her thighs. He laid a hand on her pelvic bone and began to softly caress her little bud of pleasure with his thumb, rubbing it gently in a slow, circular motion.

The restrained girl's need filled her. The hand that tormented her clit was sending streams of warm, pleasurable sensations through her loins. Drabik's cock maintained a constant motion, a slow, tantalizing rhythm. The man watched as the girl's body began to tremble and shudder in her heat. He leaned over and took a stiff nipple in his mouth, sucking gently, swirling his tongue around the wide, dark areola. Maddy groaned. Her hips were bucking now, in time with the insistent cock in her womb. Her ankles strained at her bonds, this time, not for the purpose of denying her tormentor access to her loins, but, rather, to draw him further into her needy crevasse.

Maddy felt her heat grow higher and higher. Her whole body convulsed when her orgasm began. She called out her ecstatic pleasure. Drabik felt her fleshy tunnel contract around his cock, as pulse after pulse of pleasure rocked the girl's body. He waited until her climax had diminished to a lingering echo before he began to seek his own pleasure in earnest. Maddy felt the steel hard cock drive deeper insider her. The man's hips drove into her with each rapid thrust. She wanted him to stop; she tried to beg him to stop. She squirmed and struggled at her confinements. The hard sword of flesh was driving her to almost unendurable pleasure. When Drabik felt his cock begin to throb, he rammed it home, his body stiffening. His hands were on Maddy's breasts and he squeezed them tightly as jolt after jolt of mind blowing pleasure passed through him. Maddy screamed as her intense, exquisite contractions began anew. The two bodies pressed hard at their coital connection in a mutual effort to drive the pulsing cock deeper and deeper inside her.

When his passion was expended, Drabik stood still, gathering his senses. Maddy, too, struggled to clear her pleasure befogged mind. She was still languishing in the afterglow of her climax when she felt the man withdraw his softening prick from within her. She heard him zipper his pants and sensed him stepping back. She heard the door to her stall open and close. He was gone.

Slowly, Maddy's mind returned to the grim circumstances of her reality. She could hear other women being administered to in other stalls, the hissing of showers, the shuffling of booted feet. Her and there, she heard the unmistakable sound of a human female in passion. Suddenly she realized that her powerful exclamations of lust must have been heard throughout the barn. Her public display of unbridled need filled her with shame. She tried to crawl inside her self, to shrink away. Mortification overwhelmed her.

As Maddy sat perched on the board, her legs splayed wide, she allowed herself to be carried away on a wave of self pity and fear. She could hear heavy boots pass by the door to her stall and various other activity all around her, the business of a ponygirl stable. She realized that, open and exposed as she was, any man who cared to swing open the doors to her stall would have ready access to her womb. Somehow she knew that was why her trainer had left her this way.

It was a while before anyone came. The door to her stall opened and Maddy heard two unfamiliar voices approach her. She tried, but she could not lower her head enough to see their faces. She felt rough hands on her thighs, other hands caressing her breasts. She moaned in despair as she prepared for her body to be invaded once more. A hand began to tease her slit. She tried to draw herself away, but succeeded only in being a source of amusement to the men. The disconsolate girl moaned as the fingers of the unknown hand entered her. All she could see from the angle of her perch was the criss-crossed, dark, wooden beams above her. She stared up at them disconsolately. Lips seized one of her breasts. The insistent tongue lavished attention on her stiff nipple, making her sigh.

Legs leaned up against the rail on which she lay and the prostrate girl felt the tip of a cock press at her womb's entrance. She protested futilely through the confinement in her mouth. The cruel appurtenance to her new, lowly status, allowed sounds to emerge, but not words. Her pleas for mercy came out as "Gaaaaaaa! Gaaaaaaa!" As the anonymous cock sank deeper and deeper into her, she groaned and shook in helpless rebellion. One of the men laughed. When the hard cock began its rhythmic assault, to Maddy's dismay, she felt the tingle of unwanted pleasure recommence.

The restrained girl lost count of how many men fucked her that night. She did not even know whether any of them had fucked her more than once, because she couldn't see them. Most of the men took her without regard for her own pleasure, pistoning their anonymous members inside her sheath until they had shot their load. But others languished in her pussy, stroked the little nub of pleasure at the top, caressed and sucked on her breasts, until the defenseless girl was returned to a state of frenzy. Each time she came, she cursed herself, cursed her wanton lust, cursed the men who were abusing her and cursed fate for her unhappy predicament.

It was dark when Drabik came to release her. Her pussy was sore and the results of untold ejaculations ran out of her. When Drabik brought her to her feet, she could barely stand. He dragged her to the water hose and, making her squat, washed her loins and legs. Adding a special nozzle to the hose, he washed out her sex with a cold jet of water. Maddy was grateful for that. She couldn't stand the thought of all those men's spunk lying inside her through the night. She looked up at Drabik and realized the irony of her being grateful for anything that this man did. He was her chief tormentor. He had tied her up, displayed and available for all comers. Why should she be grateful to him for anything?

Drabik toweled off his charge and led her to a narrow, thin, cotton pallet on the floor next to the side of the stall. He forced her to lay on it, on her back, while he bound her ankles and thighs with tight, wide straps. Maddy struggled with discomfort as her bound arms behind her caused her back to arch. There were rings on the floor on both sides of the 'head' of the primitive bed, and Drabik fastened a short chain from each to rings on the side of the newly minted ponygirl's collar. He also fastened her ankles to similar rings at the foot of the bed.

Satisfied that the blue hooded ponygirl was immobile, he removed the bit that was still held firmly between her teeth. It was replaced by a thick, leather probe that filled her mouth and was attached to a leather belt. The belt was fastened behind her head. The last thing that he did before he walked away was to lower small tabs with Velcro on each side over the holes for her eyes. During the day, the Velcro allowed the tabs to be up so that the pony could see to her necessary tasks. At night, it was lowered and fixed firmly in place so that the pony's sense of isolation would increase. Maddy shuddered as she was blinded again. Drabik made a final check on all of her bindings and left.

Maddy could hear her trainer's heavy boots as he navigated the warren of stalls on his way out of the barn. She heard the door of the barn roll open and closed. After that, there was an almost ghostly silence. She lay there, reveling in the quietude, grateful that her horrid day of shock and torment was at an end. Although she was trussed up cocoon-like, blinded, gagged, and anchored in place like some wayward pleasure craft, a wave of relief flowed through her. At first dismayed at her return to utter darkness, she slowly came to realize that the pitch blackness that she saw from behind her hood put a wall between her and all that had happened to her that day. It seemed more remote, less plausible somehow. Something she could bear, could think about without panic and fear.

She was exhausted from her ordeals and relished the almost dead silence of the barn. She could hear the building creak on its ancient foundations, the rustle of a neighboring nameless and faceless ponygirl as she struggled to get comfortable in her bonds. She was finally at peace, at rest. She had survived the harsh travails of her day. She let the feel of her own breathing sooth her.

And then she heard footsteps. Heavy boots walked slowly along the hallway outside her stall. She had a moment of terror as she heard the booted steps approach her door. Had someone come for her? Was her torment to begin anew? Her heart began to pound wildly, her body shuddered in fear. But the footsteps passed her door and began to fade.

The sound of the boots that Maddy heard from inside her dark, confined world underscored to her her complete and utter helplessness. That mere boot steps could render her into a state of terror spoke volumes about the new life that she was now apparently condemned to lead. Frustrated and afraid, disconsolate at her fate, she twisted and strained at her bonds and started to cry. Was there no way out of this hellish place, she thought, miserably. What would the man do to her tomorrow? But she already knew what he would do. He would make her run and run and run until she had no breath left. He would whip her when she faltered and failed to keep the relentless pace. He would make her suck his long, thick cock, the instrument that had driven her to pleasure this very night,

She knew as well that her body would be open to any who cared to use it. Her breasts and belly would be naked for all to see. How would she ever bear it, she thought forlornly. How would she survive?

But that was tomorrow. She tried to put it out of her mind; to instead take stock of herself, to see what part of her was left, was still hers.

Maddy was surprised that the loss of the use of her hands had not affected her as much as she would have thought. True, she was helpless without her hands; she couldn't open a door, unfasten a belt, scratch an itch. But she hardly thought about them throughout the day. They were behind her, out of sight. It was almost as if they didn't exist.

But her voice, the ability to speak, that was something else. She had barely said a word since she had been kidnapped, ten, or was it twelve days ago, she really didn't know anymore. During that time she had gone from a happy, laughing, carefree young woman at the height of her youth and freedom, to a dumb animal upon which anything could be imposed and from whom everything was demanded. As long as she could not speak, as long as they kept from her the right to protest and assert her humanity, she would be merely another ponygirl, a beast of burden.

After a while, Maddy's mind began to drift freely in her enforced darkness as her need for sleep overcame her. The boot steps of the watchman echoed faintly from the other side of the building like the steady drip of a faucet. She allowed the sound to mesmerize her, lull her. But, just as she was about to fall into desperately desired slumber, the steps came inexorably closer again. When she heard them reenter the corridor outside her stall, her heart began to beat in her chest like a drum, her stomach turned inside out. And then he passed by again, leaving her once more alone with her thoughts.

As her fear subsided, Maddy could not help but recall the abuses her body had been put to that day. She thought back to her whipping. Her trainer had made his point very effectively. At any time, he could create a world of torment and pain for her. She was helpless to prevent it or to assuage it. She knew that it would not be the only time that she would be whipped. She was smart enough to know that her trainer would want to keep the pain of the whip fresh in her mind. And it was inevitable that someday she would disappoint him, break some rule, overstep some bound. The rack of whips she had stared at, kneeling, her hands chained above her, while her trainer gathered her accouterments earlier that day, laid in wait for her, she just knew it.

A twitch in her right thigh muscle caused her to try and shift her weight. Her movement was automatic, a thing one would do unconsciously. But the bonds around her thighs and ankles prevented it. She had almost forgotten that she was so cruelly bound. It brought home to her the fact that she no longer had anything other than a possessory interest in her own flesh. She could occupy it, use it, motivate it to obey the commands of her masters, but she no longer owned it. It was the property of the tall, dark mustachioed man who had raped her that morning, whoever he was. If only she could put a name to him, to anyone she had seen that day, her trainer most of all. But most of her tormentors, as far as she was concerned, did not even have faces. They were anonymous agents of a regimen of harsh, intense debasement.

She remembered her now hairless sex. To her, there was no more potent symbol of her lack of control over her own body than the hewing off of her badge of sexual maturity. She was now like a child, less than a child, for even a child had some rights. And tomorrow, men would pierce it with their sexes, would lay their hands on it, probe it at will. And she would respond, shamefully, lustfully, just as she had today.

The footsteps were coming closer again. Whoever he was, he was like a ghost, haunting the warrens of the ponygirl barn. The fear returned. Maddy hated herself for it. She hated her vulnerability, her powerlessness. As the steps came closer, she whined and shifted her weight, causing a rattling of the chains that were holding her in place. The noise caused the footsteps to stop. Maddy could not help herself. She began to moan in fear. He was coming! He was coming! Her heart leapt into her throat and she began to whine when she heard the door to her stall opening. She felt the man's eyes on her. She wanted desperately to disappear. She prepared herself for the sting of a whip, or the kick of a boot. Her sex burned with the knowledge that he could have it if he wanted it.

Maddy heard the man utter lowly some guttural words that she did not understand and then felt a sharp line of fiery pain across her thighs. Her body flinched and she moaned loudly in pain. The man spoke another few words in a clearly imperative tone. The door swung closed. The boots began to walk away. Maddy began to sob as the pain from the lashing slowly subsided. She cried and cried until, finally, mercifully, she fell asleep.

* * * * * * * * * * *

Jake sat at the counter of the run down diner drinking his fourth cup of the establishment's excuse for coffee. He could see through the plate glass window the entrance to the warehouse belonging to the National Uniform Company. It was Sunday and the overhead doors were all locked shut. They had had the place under surveillance for about ten days. The tracer was still on the truck they had followed back from Georgia. It was sitting inside, parked, for the time being. Twice since they had been watching, it had rolled out to the street and undertaken a long journey. The first had been to a small town in Ohio, another remote country road, another long, gravel driveway. As before, it had stayed for maybe an hour and then was on its way back to New Jersey again.

The second trip was even longer, all the way to Michigan. This had been an urban pick up, in downtown Detroit, two days out and two days back. The truck pulled into the garage of the National Uniform Company and did not come out.

Since then, there had been no activity. From the video they had gotten on the day of Herman and Louise's summary execution, they had been able to pick up the two men who had been in the truck when they emerged from the company warehouse. The younger one had a condo down in Liberty Harbor. It was registered to a Charles Wadowski. The older guy lived in a split story ranch in Short Hills. Kids, little league, the little woman, the whole works. The house came back as owned by James and Ruth Feeney.

Burnham, Madeline's tycoon uncle, had been putting pressure on Jake for some action. Jake wanted to wait until they had the whole set up down pat. He still didn't know how they were getting the girls out. He didn't have long to wait.

Martinez called him on his cell phone and let him know that the young guy, Wadowski, was on the move. Leon called a few moments later and let him know that Feeney had left his house and was heading east, towards Elizabeth. Maybe today was the day. Jake alerted the rest of his crew. The two times they had seen a van leave the basement entrance to the warehouse it had been nighttime. Maybe something was up.

Feeney blew down 280 East to the Turnpike and got off at the Elizabeth exit. The Yanks were on the radio and were leading 2 to 1 in the fourth. Feeney had a little money on the spring training game. Nothing special, just for entertainment's sake. He pulled up to the warehouse about 3:30. As was his habit, he took a good look around before he opened the warehouse door. Chuckie was due soon. The rest of the boys would be there in an hour or so. It would take Chuckie just about that time to scoot out to the trucking company's loading dock where he would pick up ten gleaming, silver, coffin-like tubes. By the time he got back, they would be ready to load the girls into them and take them back to the loading dock for transfer to an air cargo container.

He would be sorry to see the two beach bunnies that he had picked up in Tennessee go. He didn't let any of the other men use the merchandise. They had to be satisfied with Allison, their permanent fuck toy. But he did what he pleased and he had a good time watching the two tanned beauties learn to lick pussy while Allison sucked his cock. They were both accomplished cock suckers too. He liked to watch their eyes wide with fright as they took his discharge in their mouths. But today was to be bye bye for them and all the other girls. There would be a new crop in a few days.

Jake had left the diner and Irving had taken his place. Tucker joined Jake in his Lumina. They watched Chuckie enter the warehouse and come out a few minutes later, driving the van. He was alone in it. Jake followed.

The van pulled up to a freight depot located about three miles from the airport. Jake watched the van pull into a loading dock and saw the door to the dock open. He could just see inside the freight facility through the gap between the side of the van and the open door. He was surprised to see cardboard boxes of what he presumed to be uniforms unloaded. He caught a glimpse of a silver container, long and sleek being loaded on. He counted four, but assumed that there were more. The cartons were loaded back on the truck and Chuckie pulled away. The truck went back to the National warehouse and disappeared inside.

Irving reported two more men having arrived while Chuckie was gone. They watched the warehouse for about an hour and a half. The van emerged at about 6 p.m. Chuckie was driving again, but the older guy, Feeney, was with him.

Jake and Irving followed the van back to the freight depot. This time there was a flatbed truck with an air cargo container on it. After about ¾ of an hour, the flatbed took off, followed by the van a few minutes later. Jake decided to follow the flatbed. It went straight to the airport. They watched it enter the freight yard.

"Can you trace that thing?" Jake asked Irving.

"Easy," Irving replied. "I got the cargo number of the container. Get me back to the hotel and I can have its destination in about ten minutes."

Jake called in all the troops. They met at the hotel, Jake's room, which was a suite and had a conference table in it. Jake called for opinions.

Martinez spoke first. "Why don't we pick up this Feeney guy and go to work on him? Tucker'll have him singing in a half an hour."

"And what if he dummies up?" Jake asked. "If he goes missing, the whole operation could disappear. We need to know for sure where he's sending the girls."

Irving came in from his room. "I've got it," he said. "The container is shipping via a company known as Fertivo Transport. It's an old mob front. The destination is a small country called Kalikastan. It's in the former Soviet Union."

Leon spoke up. "I've heard of that place. It's wild west city."

"I know it too," Jake said. "It's damn hard to get into. It's run by local mobs. If Madeline's there, she'll be hard as hell to find."

"What if we find out who picks up the container?" Irving asked.

"That'll tell us who's taking delivery," Jake answered. "But that wouldn't be her final destination. She's probably been sold to someone else, a private collector or a whorehouse." Jake paused to think about the import of his remarks. He had a vision of that happy, smiling, young woman he had seen in the pictures in her apartment being used as somebody's private sex slave, or worse yet, fucking twenty men a day in a brothel. Either way, the girl's life would be a nightmare.

"Everybody agrees that Maddy probably went out on one of these containers?" Jake asked. There was general assent. "O.K.," he said. "I'll call Burnham."

CHAPTER TWELVE

Maddy was awoken by the sound of the barn's sliding door. She panicked, at first, to find herself in total darkness, but she recalled quickly where she was and what had been done to her. She wondered what time it was. The activity in the barn picked up slowly. She could hear other ponygirls being released from their night bonds, the sound of hands slapping flesh, the distinctive patter of running water. She had to pee badly and prayed that someone would come for her before she found it necessary to empty her bladder. It would be just one more humiliation to be found lying in puddle of piss when the man came to release her.

She did not have to wait long, however. She heard the door to her stall open and sensed someone kneeling by her side. Her ankles and thighs were freed and the chains affixing her in her sleeping position were released. A strong hand helped her regain her feet. She was still blinded and so could not see who was handling her, but she was sure it was not the man from the day before. She felt herself being tugged over to the corner of the stall, over the drain, and hands on her shoulders encouraged her to squat. She released her flow of water gratefully.

When she stood, after being wiped, the strong hands forced her to sit on a bench. Her boots were put on and she was stood up and led from her stall. When she reached the common area, the tabs over her eyes were pulled up. She could see that the other ponygirls were being brought out of their stalls as well. The door to the barn opened and the ponygirls surged towards the entrance. Maddy looked around and saw the grizzled face of the man who had awoken her. It was not her trainer after all. He smiled at her and slapped her bare buttocks, as if to urge her on.

Maddy took the hint and began to follow the other naked, bound, blue hooded ponygirls. They were following the pathway that led from the barn, up a little hill and to the vast open area she had seen the day before. It was strange to be unescorted, but Maddy knew that she should go with the herd. There were twenty seven ponygirls at the Grobgy farm, including Maddy. Maddy saw them all assembling at the entrance to the large, round, wide track that she had seen the day before. Rough looking men had aggregated there. Maddy could see through the dime sized holes in her mask the other ponies stretching their legs, running in place. She wondered what it was all about. There was a short whistle and the ponygirls crowded together at the entrance to the track, their blue heads at alert. Maddy tried to close in as well. When the second whistle blew, the ponygirls all took off like a shot.

Maddy was taken aback by the surge forward of the other ponies. After a moment, she realized that they had been brought out for a morning run and, by the way the other ponygirls had taken off, there must be some consequence to how one finished the race. Panicking that she had such a late start, Maddy took off desperately after the other naked females.

Drabik watched the poor, newly minted ponygirl stumble ahead. She was obviously nowhere near used to running with her hands bound behind her as the other animals. Moreover, she was still gagged, and needed to take in all of her oxygen through her nose. That and her late start, not to mention her woefully inadequate physical condition, condemned her to finish last.

It may have been unfair to not give Maddy the benefit of knowing that she was queuing up for a race, but it was part of the training regimen not to give the ponygirls any unnecessary verbal instructions. They would learn commands, mostly one or two word ones such as 'kneel' and 'bend over', all spoken in Russian. But ponygirls were never talked to. Why should they be? They had lost their humanity. One might as well have a conversation with a horse. They would learn to obey hand signals, claps, even the sound of a mechanical cricket. The point was to erode away their natural instinct for language, to render them reactive, instead of contemplative. As the weeks and months went by, the trainees found themselves searching for words in their minds, standing virtually empty headed at times. They were intended to stop thinking of themselves as women and, instead, think of themselves as merely intelligent, beautiful chattel.

Maddy saw the line of hooded, naked females distancing themselves from her, their pony tails dancing in the wind behind them. She was running as fast as she could, but her legs were not strong enough to propel her as quickly as the others. She had kept up a good sprint for the first hundred yards or so, but her speed quickly faltered. The track was about 9/10ths of a mile long, 1500 meters. The finish line was a complete mile from the start, some 100 yards past the point of beginning.

By the time Maddy had rounded the far turn, the other former women were far ahead of her. She plodded on desperately, knowing full well that she was doomed to finish last and suffer whatever consequences that brought. As the white fence streamed by her, she thought momentarily of trying to jump it, to try to run away. But she knew that she would only bring further suffering down on herself.

When Maddy finally reached the end, the other ponygirls had already pretty much recovered their breaths.

Maddy had to lean over to try and gain control of her heaving chest. She heard men around her laughing. The other ponies silently began the trek back to the barn. Maddy tried to join them but was waylaid by two pairs of strong hands. She was dragged over to a horizontal rail, about three feet off of the ground and supported by two wooden posts. Her torso was pushed over the rail and a strap was attached to her collar and then tied off to a ring that was embedded in the ground between the two posts. Her legs were spread and tied off as well.

Maddy realized that she was about to be whipped. Nothing was done around here without a purpose, and her posture made her ass and legs ready for the whip. She could feel her bare labial lips spread wide and knew that she could not expect to leave her post without its availability taken advantage of.

The girl pledged to herself that she would not wail or cry. She would absorb the blows stoically. But when the first fiery trail was lashed across her buttocks, all of her resolve left her. "Please don't, please!" she tried to wail. But her words were stifled by her gag. Five sturdy strokes with a switch was the punishment for finishing last, and Maddy screamed and yelled at each blow. She had thought that she had survived the worst yesterday, but now knew that her travails could worsen at any moment. She also realized that she would suffer many morning lashings until she was in shape enough to truly compete with the other ponygirls.

When the five lashes had been administered, Maddy lay whimpering over the post. A hand slapped her rear and then descended between her thighs. She stiffened as she felt a finger probe her naked slit. There was more laughter. The finger probed deeper into her gash, stroking it along its length, pushing past the tender lips. When the finger found her little bud of pleasure, Maddy whined, knowing what would soon follow. The finger tickled the little nubbin until Maddy's sex began to secrete its lubrication. When two fingers, soaked in her rising juices, pressed inwards, Maddy could not suppress a moan.

When the first cock entered her, Maddy felt a surge of revulsion and shame. Her head was pulled down and all she could see through the little holes in her hood was two khaki covered legs between hers. Hands that she could not see grabbed her hips and used them to leverage their owner's cock deeper inside her. When her passage was fully flushed and relaxed, the cock began a steady rasp against her clit and the sides of her sex.

Maddy had not yet reached her peak of pleasure when the first cock exploded its hot cream into her pussy. When the second cock began to throb and pulse, Maddy was in heat, rocking her hips to maximize her rising lust. It was when the third cock filled her that Maddy's need for climax became acute. She rocked her body back and forth on the post, frantically driving herself to pleasure. She began to moan and cry behind her gag. The men around her sensed her coming climax and they urged her assailant on. As the third man jetted a stream of cum inside her, Maddy came, her pussy clamping down on its possessor, squeezing it tight. Wave after wave of pleasure went through her as she received the unknown man's hot flood.

The fun must have gone out of the game, because no fourth cock assailed her dripping sex. She saw the legs of the men leaving as she tried to regain her breath. She became afraid that the men would leave her there all day. But her fear grew to terror when she saw the face of her trainer lean down between her legs.

Drabik had witnessed Maddy's abysmal performance on the track. He knew the consequences of finishing last and did not interfere when the other trainers imposed the punishment. He waited until they had taken their pleasure with her, as was their right, before approaching his bent over charge. When he bent down, he stared menacingly at the two little holes in the hood. He reached out and grabbed the nipples of the ponygirl's downward pointing breasts and squeezed hard. Maddy felt a jolt of pain in her breasts that made her gasp. She had disappointed her trainer. Now he would inflict his own punishment.

The man loosened Maddy's legs and drew them together. He hooked her tall, black boots to each other. When he stood, he unraveled a long, thick strap. Without any ceremony, he struck the ponygirl across the back of her joined thighs.

The impact of the broad belt of leather striking Maddy's flesh made a loud 'crack!' Maddy seethed with pain. Another blow followed, this one higher up, at the base of her buttocks. It made another loud 'crack!' Drabik waited patiently until the results of each blow subsided before applying another. Maddy was crying now desperately. She tried to beg him to stop, to promise a better result tomorrow, to endeavor to do her best, but the words were just a jumble of sounds through her gag, interwoven with her moans and cries at the landing of each blow.

Maddy didn't know how many times that the man whipped her, but she was overwhelmed with relief when it ended. She felt her ankles unbound and the strap between her collar and the ring in the ground released. Drabik pulled her to an upwards position by her pony tail. He quickly pushed her to her knees. The significance of his action was not lost on the ponygirl. She waited forlornly as he released her gag and extracted his thick cock from his pants. She was to reward her tormentor. She meekly opened her mouth and seized on the tumescent flesh. Whipping a ponygirl always made Drabik hard.

The stiff pole filled Maddy's mouth. She tightened her grip on it with her lips and pulled her head back, giving the man's cock a long, hot stroke. The freshly dehumanized ponygirl could not help be conscious of the increasing activity around them as men and women began to go about their daily business. She imagined in her mind what they could see as she ran her tongue around the tip of Drabik's dick: a faceless, supine, abject female serving her master.

Drabik allowed the ponygirl to suck him at her own pace. He rested his hands lightly on her head as she bobbed back and forth. The female had skills, he gave her that. Some of the new ponygirls had to whipped and beaten until they learned to suck a cock right. But this one knew her business. He moaned as her lips and tongue inflamed him. Her efforts were slow, but relentless. The warmth of her mouth spread through him. As his passion rose, he resisted the urge to press her head down, to force himself down her throat. He wanted all of the effort to be hers.

Maddy could feel the telltale signs of Drabik's climax approach. She withdrew her mouth and caressed the tip of his cock with her tongue. When she heard the man groan, she encircled the bulbous head of his manhood with her lips and urged the orgasm on with her tongue. She had just the end of his cock in her mouth when the first spurt of hot cum was released. She received his discharge dutifully, encouraging each pulse and spasm. As the cock began to spurt in earnest, she pressed her lips forward, taking the cock deep into her mouth, spreading the heat of her mouth over its length.

Intense pleasure shot through Drabik's body as he enjoyed the benefits of Maddy's efforts. His grip on her head became hard as he groaned at each throbbing spurt of his cum. The ponygirl did not relent her efforts until his cock had concluded its pleasurable spasms and he had begun to soften in her mouth.

Drabik recovered possession of his tool from the young female's mouth. "She's clever," he thought. "She thinks that a good blow job will soften me." She was wrong. But she did set a high standard for herself. One by which future blow jobs would be measured. After restoring the gag, he grabbed the ring of her collar and pulled her to her feet. He said nothing to her, merely began to walk back to the barn. Maddy understood that she was to follow and did so, the taste of his sperm still in her mouth.

Maddy was fed and allowed to void. Her trainer removed her hood and, keeping her face turned away from him, shaved her head, removing any stubble that had grown in the last two days. He then, after restoring her hood, shaved her pudenda. Maddy was to learn that this was a daily ritual. Each day, her trainer or someone appointed by him, would make sure that she remained hairless but for the stream of auburn hair that jutted from the back of her hood and then descended down her back. Once she had been fully outfitted as a ponygirl, her day would also begin with a ritualistic enforcement of an orgasm upon her, to remind her of the subservience of all of her body's functions to her masters.

When he finished feeding and shaving her, Drabik took her back out to the sand pit for more exercise. He replaced the gag with her bit and hooked her back to the revolving pole. The unhappy ponygirl grunted as the pole relentlessly tugged her forward. She had a new dedication to her task. She was determined to strengthen her legs, increase her endurance. Although it might take some time, she did not intend to be last in the daily, ritual run for long.

Drabik watched the ponygirl add a spring to her step as she followed the lead of the mechanical pole. He watched her actually get ahead of it, creating slack in the chain that connected her to it. But that was not good either. Ponygirls did not think for themselves. Ponygirls obeyed. And if the pace was a trot, then the ponygirl trotted. Drabik lashed out at Maddy's buttocks with the switch. She yelled as the lash bit her. She was mystified, at first, at what she had done wrong, but after the third remonstrance with the whip, she realized that she was being ordered to maintain the pace of the lead and no more. Dutifully, she slowed until the pole began to tug at her bit.

During the three hours that Drabik kept her at her paces, Maddy had much time to think. She appreciated the purpose of the daily race and the motivational beating and rape. It was working with her. She considered the alternative to obedience, the consequences of lagging in her efforts or refusal to react to commands. But her fear of pain was stronger than her urge for dignity. Wouldn't they just destroy her, ultimately, like they would an intractable horse? They would put her down, she surmised, and not humanely with a shot of some painless potion, or a bullet to the back of the head. She guessed that something significantly more painful and excruciating would be called for. And before they concluded that she was a truly lost cause, she would have to suffer all the torments and pain that would be inflicted in an effort to 'correct' her attitude. No, she would obey. And if avoidance of pain was not a sufficient motivator, she wanted to live. She refused to believe that this was to be her permanent condition. Someday, she would escape. She felt it in her bones.

And so round and round the track she went. She trotted when the pole was slow, galloped when the pole went faster and sprinted when it reached its highest speed.

Drabik watched the ponygirl put in her extra effort. There was a noticeable difference in her performance today than yesterday. She only fell once, and then she lifted herself back up and resumed running. The ponygirl had spirit all right. She just might be a winner.

When they broke for lunch, Maddy was taken back into the barn, showered and fed. Drabik leaned her against the board face down and massaged her legs. Maddy languished in the soothing sensations of the massage. She had done well; she knew it. She pledged to work harder that afternoon.

After finishing the massage, Drabik stood Maddy up, her waist against the rail. He buckled her boots to rings in the floor and fastened a chain from her bit to the wall in front of her. He patted her on the rump, gently and then left.

The ponygirl wondered why she had been left there. Yesterday, they had resumed her exercise right after lunch break. Was something different going to happen today?

It was while pondering this thought that Maddy remembered the nose rings the other ponygirls wore. She cringed inwardly at the thought of being defaced in this manner. She knew it was inevitable and that all the other ponygirls had suffered similar fates. But that did not change her own horror at the prospect of bearing the dehumanizing appurtenance.

While musing on her fate, Maddy went over the morning's events in her mind. It was the first real chance she had to examine the bodies of the other ponygirls up close and she remarked now at what she had failed to remark then. It suddenly occurred to her that each of the ponygirls had some form of writing stenciled in blue upon their chests. Could it have been a tattoo? Maddy cursed the restrictions on her vision. She could barely see anything well. Her heart fell as she realized that they must have been tattoos. Since the ponygirls all looked so much alike, they must tattoo their names on their chests. She pulled at her ankle bindings nervously and began to whine. She didn't want to be tattooed. She wanted to go home. She wanted to be released. Her few moments of tranquility, brought on by the natural endorphins from her intense exercise and her trainer's massage was destroyed. She didn't want to be a ponygirl. She began to cry.

Drabik had in fact been making arrangements for Maddy's markings. Her limited vision had prevented her from noticing the rampant yellow wolf, the symbol from the Grobgy crest, tattooed on the loins of the other ponygirls, just above their sexes. It was the mark of their training estate. Each estate had its own distinctive mark. Grobgy had adopted the fierce looking wolf as a sign of his own ferocity. It was a symbol well deserved.

The tattooist had a small building located on the edge of the circle of buildings that made up the Grobgy estate. As with others, the man had many functions. Tattooing ponygirls was one of them. He spoke briefly with Drabik, got his instructions for the tattoo of Maddy's new name and made his preparations. He then left to retrieve the new ponygirl.

Maddy heard the door to her stall open. She felt her boots being released and then saw a man dressed in a salmon colored work shirt and blue jeans step in front of her and disconnect the chain from the wall. As he began to lead her from her stall, Maddy pulled back on the leash. She was beside herself with fear. Wherever this man was taking her, she did not want to go. The man grabbed her leash near to her neck and pulled it upwards, causing Maddy to rise onto her toes. With his other hand, he pulled a quirt from his belt and struck Maddy in the legs three times. Maddy screamed and struggled to avoid the blows. When he was done, the man began to tug her from her stall. Maddy gave up her resistance and followed him.

Once outside the barn, the man let the leash extend and pulled Maddy behind him as he walked. They were proceeding along a long path of reddish bricks. Maddy took the opportunity to take as good a look around as she could, as well as could be done given her restrictive collar and the tiny eyeholes in her hood. She saw the paddock and the track she had run on that morning, the magnificent house on the hill. There were stables for actual, real horses and a kennel for dogs. Vast fields of grass surrounded the buildings of the estate and a lone, gravel road led away from it and over a nearby hill. The estate was located in a small valley and rough terrain surrounded it on all sides. There was enough room for wheat and soybean fields, and a large grassy area, fenced in, so that the horses could run and exercise when not in use.

Maddy saw the small building to which they were heading. It was made of brown clapboard with a peaked roof. She was led up three steps and then through the white, windowless door. There were no windows in the building and it was dark inside until the man flicked the switch that brightened it. Maddy saw a chair sitting in the middle of the cabin's only room. The man who had led her there pushed Maddy down onto it.

Maddy's eyes started to tear as she realized that she was about to be subjected to some kind of procedure. She did not resist, however, as the man strapped her in. Tight straps went around her torso above and below her belly button. The back of her collar was locked into place by a clip to the ring there. More straps fixed her legs in place, spreading them widely and holding her thighs tightly against the sides of the chair. Her arms were pressed into the back of the chair beneath her. The man turned away from the ponygirl to a counter with various tools strewn about it.

It was the man's habit to start with the tattooing. It was painful and tedious and so better to get it done first, when the female was still fresh. He went to work almost at once. Maddy recognized the tattoo gun. Her friend had one done once, a little bluebird on her shoulder blade. This tattoo, she knew, would be much more prominent.

Maddy stiffened as the gun made its first puncture of skin. She gritted her teeth against her bit to fight off the pain. The man had insinuated himself between her widespread legs, and she could see the top of his head as he concentrated on his task. He was done with the chest in about thirty minutes. He then went back to his counter to change ink and pick up a stencil. He pulled a little stool between Maddy's legs and washed her stomach with alcohol. Maddy had no idea of what the man was up to. She squirmed slightly as the ink gun pierced the skin of her belly. The man sat back on the stool, looking her in the eye. He reached a hand down between her legs and grabbed her clit between forefinger and thumb, the same way that Drabik had grabbed her. He squeezed hard. Maddy squirmed and moaned in pain. She nodded her head to signal her acquiescence in his procedure. Her clit was released and the man recommenced his work.

When he was finished, a large, yellow wolf, its paws reaching out aggressively, its mouth pulled back in a snarl, adorned Maddy's stomach. This would mark her as one of Grobgy's ponygirls. Even if sold later, this mark would denote her as coming from his stables and a product of his training staff. The man admired the decorative scroll on Maddy's chest. "*молния*", "Lightning", Maddy's new name.

Now came the difficult part. At least it would be difficult for Maddy. Her legs were spread wider and lifted up slightly and the back of the chair was lowered. The man didn't like the ponygirls to see what was to be done before he started and he concealed the nature of his tools from Maddy. Maddy's head was back now and the angle of her collar and the tiny holes in her hood prevented her from seeing what the man was doing. Suddenly, she felt a sharp, excruciating pain in her nether lip. Her whole body spasmed and she yelled out fiercely. A second, tearing type pain was felt by the former young woman and she shook and moaned. Two thick golden rings had been set onto piercings made in her labia. They were low enough not to interfere with the enjoyment of her cunt, designed mostly to provide a easy way to affix the ponygirl to a leash, or to bind her to a post. They also carried small golden discs that were engraved with the name and emblem of her current ownership. While her tattoo would never be removed, the discs could easily be replaced if she was sold.

The man mopped up the blood with a cotton ball and applied styptic to the wounds he had opened. Maddy's eyes teared as she felt the sting of the astringent on her nether lips.

Next came the nose ring. The man stepped from between Maddy's legs and took some pads from the counter. They locked in place on either side of Maddy's head, imprisoning it. Maddy knew what was coming and, involuntarily, began to whine. "I am not an animal!" she thought to herself frantically. "I am not an animal!"

The piercing of the nose was less painful than the piercing of the labial lips. Maddy uttered a short groan when the inside of her nose was pierced. A golden ring was placed through the hole. The ring was large enough to rest on her upper lip. Maddy could feel its heavy weight there.

The man placed an asbestos sheet between Maddy's upper lip and the ring and soldered its ends closed. Maddy could feel the heat of the soldering gun as it was applied to the ring only millimeters from her skin. The man waited until the ring had cooled and then turned it so that the soldered end was in Maddy's nose. He stood back to admire his work. She looked wonderful.

After cleaning up his tools, the man released Maddy from her chair. There were no mirrors in the little cabin, so she still had no idea what she looked like. There was little time to ruminate over what the man had done to her, as he reaffixed her leash to her bit and led her back outside.

The whole procedure had taken about an hour and a half. The sun was midway between its zenith and the horizon. The tattoos needed to be kept out of the sun to prevent the ink from fading. It would be okay in a day or so. But until then, Maddy's exercises would be confined to early morning and late afternoons.

Maddy shuffled behind the man helplessly. Her loins and nose still ached from her piercings and her chest and belly burned. Once they reached the barn, the man rolled the door open and brought the poor ponygirl in. He slid the door closed and presented Maddy to the tall mirror that was affixed there to the wall.

Maddy's heart sank as she saw herself reflected in the mirror. There were two and a half inch ornate letters inscribed across her chest in deep blue. On her belly she could see the body of the wolf that she had seen on the crest over the barn door. It was outlined in black to increase its visibility. Two little, glittering rings hung from her sex and a larger, shiny, golden hued ring descended from her nose, contrasting sharply with the deep blue of her head and face encompassing hood. She was now a marked and decorated beast.

The tattooist pushed down on Maddy's shoulders. She realized that he was ordering her to her knees for a particular purpose. She sank to the ground, despondent at her new physical attributes and the mean fate that had befallen her. She felt her bit removed and opened her mouth mechanically. When the man pierced her lips with his hardened meat, her stomach turned in revulsion. The man who had so cruelly pierced her and had so callously marked her was in her mouth. She was to pleasure him, to reward him for his fine work. Maddy had the urge to try and spit out the unwanted intruder, but she remembered his easy use of the quirt when he had taken her from the pony barn and the fierce grasp of her loins he had taken when she had tried to avoid being marked.

Propelled by fear of pain, Maddy turned her attention to pleasuring the steel like rod that filled her mouth. The man had a grasp of her pony tail and was pumping her head over his cock. It struck the back of her throat, gagging her. She tried her best to pleasure the instrument with her lips and tongue, but the man sought only the confines of her throat for his pleasure. His hand pushed her head down onto his lower belly, causing the thick meat to intrude into Maddy's throat. She could not breathe, but resisted pulling away. She knew that she could not assuage what she had to endure and that struggling only made it worse. Frankly, she was so despondent she cared little if she choked to death.

She did not choke to death, as the man's orgasm came quickly. His cock was still spurting as he drew it out, and he let the last few spasms of his tool jet his hot, sticky cum onto Maddy's breasts. While the man stuffed his cock back into his pants, Maddy turned to her right to take another look at herself in the mirror. Only the fact that the image's movements matched her own could convince her that what she saw was really her. The gold ring in her nostrils gleamed, even in the dull light of the barn. The large Cyrillic letters shouted out her new identity.

The man took her back to her stall and restored her to her former position. This time, however, he turned her back to the rail and affixed the back of her collar to the wall. She stood, legs apart, presented to anyone who deigned to come into her stall. The man kissed her breasts, sucking hard on the nipples until they were hard and the ponygirl moaned. He then patted her face and left.

Maddy stood, in presentation position, for about two hours. She could hear various goings on in the barn, none of which concerned her. The aching of her piercings had reduced to mere throbs. The burning of her tattoos was receding. But the hurt that was deep inside her would not diminish. She knew that soon her trainer would come through the door that she had been studying without surcease for two hours. He would do with her body what he pleased. She would obey him without question.

When Drabik finally arrived, he was carrying a large mirror. He hung it on the back of the stall door. Maddy could see her reflection clearly. She had not changed. Drabik circled behind her, ducking under the railing that pressed against her back. He stood so that she could see his face hanging over her shoulder. His hands came around from behind her and grasped her soft, ample breasts. Maddy could see the large, scarred hands in the mirror as they gently caressed her plush, twin globes. He pinched at her nipples, just enough to cause them to stand up. Maddy felt his hot lips on her shoulder.

"No, no, no!" Maddy said to herself. He was going to make her watch herself come. She could already feel the tingle of passion in her loins. His arm encircled her waist, taking care not to press on the newly applied tattoo of her owner's crest. Drabik massaged the breasts, moving his free hand from one to the other. He placed his hot hand over them and, lifting them one after the other, dug his fingers gently, but firmly, into their mass.

Maddy felt her juices begin to flow. Part of her yearned for him to lower his hand, to massage the apex of her slit, to delve deeply within her. She was mesmerized by the vision of the hands touching her, caressing her. Was it her, or some strange beast that she saw? Her lips were grotesquely spread by her cruel bit, her eyes were but tiny circles of darkness set forth on her featureless mask. She saw the strange letters denoting her new name, a name that she didn't even know, reversed in the mirror's reflection, as well as the rampant wolf, its claws held fiercely in the air, the symbol of her owner and master. What hope had a young girl against such cruelty? As her pleasure mounted against her very will, Maddy understood where her future lay. She must be what she has become: a beast, a ponygirl. All of the past was gone, there was only the present. Like an animal, feral in its nature, she could have no thought for the future.

When the man's hand flitted over her belly and began to caress the inside of her thighs, she moaned. Drabik looked up unto the mirror. He could see the signs of passion on the ponygirl, her reddened chest, the fullness of her breasts. Her hips moved as if begging him to caress the gash at the center of her thighs. He could not see her eyes, but her breathing, heavy and deep, revealed the extent of her rising desire.

He slid his hand over the now pouting lower lips. He grazed the inside of her slit with his thumb, passing lightly over her hard clit. Maddy moaned in spite of herself. Her mind was screaming 'no, no,' to this demonstration of the man's mastery over her, 'no' to this exhibition of her shameful lust. But her body celebrated the carnal contact.

Her loins burned with passion. She felt Drabik's hand return to her moist, tender channel. This time, his fingers entered her, pressing deeply within. He spread her moisture over her labia and up to the nubbin of pleasure atop her split, luscious cleft. He placed his fingers on it, rubbing it gently. Maddy hissed with pleasure, pressing her loins forward into the man's hand. She could see his hand caressing her, see his smiling, mocking face. She watched as her breasts bounced and swayed in response to the rocking of her hips. "Ohhhhhhhhhhh!" she moaned as the fingers continued to enflame her. Her knees began to buckle when the first throbs of ecstasy ran through her. She was held up by the man's hand around her waist. Drabik rubbed harder now, pressing on the hard clit. Maddy's body bucked as her orgasm overwhelmed her. The man's hand covered her hot pussy, grasping it tightly. The ponygirl pushed her loins against it, seeking and finding fulfillment.

Drabik continued to rub Maddy's pussy gently and slowly as her orgasm subsided. She looked at him in the mirror. His eyes were intent and hard. He had conveyed yet another lesson to Maddy in a most convincing way. Her body was no longer hers, but it could bring her pleasure as well as pain. Her masters would decide which.

* * * * * * * * * * *

Jake had been on the telephone with Maddy's uncle, Michael Burnham, for over an hour. He explained carefully why they couldn't go into the warehouse like gangbusters. He explained that it was taking so long because they had to be careful. These were powerful people. Kalikastan was not New York. Maddy could disappear forever. Burnham was beside himself. "You've got to get in there, Jake!" he said.

"You've got to go in and find out what has happened to her!"

"More easily said than done," Jake replied. "But, I do have a plan."

End Book One.